Why oh why was Axel Parks still in the ministry and how did he and Gia get together? Of all the people in the world to get married, why on earth did it have to be those two?

It felt surreal, and maybe it was.

Maybe it wasn't Gia Fire from college. But the surname Fire was not exactly common, and Gia was a pastor's kid. Her father had his own church called the House of Fire.

Out of the two of them, Gia or Axel, Walter had no idea whose presence would disturb him the most, but he didn't want a reappearance of either of them in his life. Now that they were together it was like a twin nightmare.

FIRE AND WALTER

BRENDA BARRETT

Fire and Walter

A Jamaica Treasures Book/May 2018

Published by Jamaica Treasures
Kingston, Jamaica

This is a work of fiction. Names, characters, places, and incidents are either the product of the author's imagination or are used fictitiously. Any resemblance to an actual person or persons, living or dead, events, or locales is entirely coincidental.

Jamaica Treasures
P.O. Box 482
Kingston 19
Jamaica W.I.
www.fiwibooks.com

ALSO BY BRENDA BARRETT

FULL CIRCLE
NEW BEGINNINGS
THE PREACHER AND THE PROSTITUTE
AFTER THE END
THE EMPTY HAMMOCK
THE PULL OF FREEDOM
REBOUND SERIES
THREE RIVERS SERIES
NEW SONG SERIES
BANCROFT SERIES
MAGNOLIA SISTERS SERIES
SCARLETT SERIES
WILEY BROTHERS SERIES

ABOUT THE AUTHOR

Books have always been a big part of life for Jamaican born Brenda Barrett, she reports that she gets withdrawal symptoms if she does not consume at least two books per week. That is all she can manage these days, as her days are filled with writing, a natural progression from her love of reading. Currently, Brenda has several novels on the market, she writes predominantly in the historical fiction, Christian fiction, comedy and romance genres.

Apart from writing fictional books, Brenda writes for her blogs blackhair101.com; where she gives hair care tips and fiwibooks.com, where she shares about her writing life.

You can connect with Brenda online at:
Brenda-Barrett.com
Twitter.com/AuthorWriterBB
Facebook.com/AuthorBrendaBarrett

Chapter One

"**H**ow can we preach redemption in our church and claim that we love people and yet the first mistake that our pastor makes, we boot him out?" Elder Donald was speaking. "It is unfair. It is unconscionable. It is unchristian!"

Walter was only half listening.

He was the newest of the twelve elders, and he was usually not very vocal in their meetings.

He had the dubious distinction of being the youngest on the board of elders, which consisted of seven males and five females. He was also unmarried and way too young and good-looking for the post.

At least that was what Sis Sinclair had declared when she heard that he was appointed.

"Pastor White was caught red-handed," Elder Cooper said in a measured tone. "He was stealing from the tithes to build a house for a church sister. He was wrong, and he only said he was sorry because he got caught."

"That's right!" Elder Mary said, "I confronted him about it, and he told me that he did not regret doing it because the church sister was poor and needed the help.

"Now I would buy his philanthropy and call him a modern Robin Hood if I didn't know for a fact that this particular church sister was rumored to be his girlfriend, his side chick, the woman on the side with our dearest first lady. There is no shame in these young church sisters game I tell you. No shame."

"Give me strength," Elder Jimmy murmured. "We do not discuss rumors in this meeting."

Elder Mary snorted. "He is a thief and an adulterer and when he said sorry he was a liar too."

"See!" Elder Donald sighed, "that is the kind of judgmental unchristian attitude, I detest."

"He is your friend." Elder Mary slapped the conference table. "And you will defend him to the end, which makes you an accessory to his crimes against this holy body. I move for Donald Green to be kicked off the board of elders."

"Come now, Elder Mary," Elder Harding the head elder said in a calm tone. "I hear your grievances and your passion. Elder Donald I admire your stance on redemption. Unfortunately, whether or not the pastor stays or goes is a decision for headquarters, and we will stand by their decision when it is made."

"I called this meeting to talk about our new pastor. He is a young man with a young wife. He recently got married."

"Young wife, that's good." Elder Mary nodded, "which means he is still in love. We need more love in our pastor's relationships. Too many of them are unhappy and looking outside of their marriages."

Elder Harding cleared his throat. "Elder Mary, please."

"I am only speaking the truth," Elder Mary said bluntly.

"Anyway," Elder Harding removed his glasses and wiped them with his handkerchief. "Our new appointee is Pastor Axel Parks, he and his wife Lady Gia Fire Parks will start with us next week."

Walter bolted up in his chair as if somebody had stuck him with a pin. There were only two names in his life that could cause that reaction. Axel Parks and Gia Fire.

Axel had almost raped him when he was seventeen and Gia was the woman who had led him astray, far down the path of sin. Some of the things he did with her he didn't even want to remember.

"Something wrong Elder Walter?" Elder Mary asked him.

Walter did not realize that he was standing at the table, while the rest of the elders were looking at him in alarm.

"I er..." Walter pondered the merits of speaking out about the pastor and his first lady.

For one, he would be sharing personal information that he did not want anyone to know about and two the elders could only recommend a pastor's dismissal. They did not hire or fire anyone.

"Excuse me a moment." Walter inhaled raggedly. "I forgot something in the car."

He almost ran out of the church conference room. What were the odds that the two most destructive people in his life were going to be his pastor and first lady?

He got in his car and sat in the driver's seat. The parking lot was nearly empty except for the elder's cars and those of a few singers. He could hear them practicing in the church hall.

They were singing one of his old favorites, Marvelous Grace, but he couldn't appreciate it, not now.

He stared at the poui tree standing like a silent sentry in the parking lot. In the days, under the tree was the coolest place to park. In the nights, it was too dark, no one cared to park there. He could see the orange blossoms glistening under the floodlights, and his eyes fell on one flower in particular. He stared at it fixatedly.

He couldn't look away from the tree. His muscles relaxed, and he retreated in his head. He wouldn't think about why he was here, sitting in the car.

His phone vibrated in his pocket, but he didn't react. His limbs were refusing to work. His hands felt weightless as if he couldn't raise them.

The phone stopped vibrating.

This was his default mode whenever he heard bad news. He thought of it as the freeze. He tried to shake himself out of it. He was older now. He was wiser. He knew hiding from situations and retreating in his head was not the way to handle his problems. He didn't need a psychiatrist to tell him that. And he had visited a psychotherapist for just this issue.

He inhaled raggedly and exhaled again. What he needed to do was go back into the meeting, apologize to the elders, and tell them he had to go home. Maybe he would see one of his brothers and tell them the devastating news.

They would eventually hear anyways, and then he would have a decision to make—stay at this church or go somewhere else because he could not envision himself attending the same church as Axel and Gia. He would have to give a reason for his departure, especially since he had just started coordinating the breakfast program, where the church catered breakfast to its members and visitors one hour before the beginning of service.

It was going so well, that church attendance and punctuality had increased exponentially. The church programs were richer. They wouldn't want to let him go as an elder anytime soon. He would have to explain.

Why oh why was Axel Parks still in the ministry and how did he and Gia get together? Of all the people in the world to get married, why on earth did it have to be those two?

It felt surreal, and maybe it was.

Maybe it wasn't Gia Fire from college. But the surname Fire was not exactly common, and Gia was a pastor's kid. Her father had his own church called the House of Fire.

Elder Harding just said Gia Fire Parks.

He knew why he stressed the Fire. They were a famous church family. And made even more popular when her father migrated to the US and started his own church, which had its own cable station, Fire TV.

Out of the two of them, Gia or Axel, Walter had no idea whose presence would disturb him the most, but he didn't want a reappearance of either of them in his life. Now that they were together it was like a twin nightmare.

He felt like just driving out of the parking lot and head home, but he changed his mind when he saw Elder Mary appear at the boardroom door. She was on her phone and looking out on the parking lot. He had already caused enough alarm with his strange behavior earlier; he should just get up and go inside.

He got out of the car and stretched, moving his head and shoulders from side to side to ease the tension between his shoulder blades.

He could do this.

Axel and Gia were just people. They had caused him problems, yes. They had marked his life, yes. But they were still just people.

The incident with Axel was ten years ago, he and Gia broke up eight years ago. His life had changed since then, and obviously, their lives had changed too.

Gia was the first lady, something she had sworn she would

never become and Axel was still a minister. Walter hoped Axel's life had taken a turn for the better through the years.

He wanted to believe that he was converted now.

Walter slammed the car door shut and walked toward the boardroom.

Elder Mary stopped him at the door. "What's wrong?"

"Nothing." Walter cleared his throat. His voice sounded rusty and unused.

Mary squinted at him as if she were trying to read his mind. "You are lying to me Elder Walter, lying lips are an abomination of the Lord and they that speak truly are his delight."

Walter groaned. Mary loved to use Bible texts to bring her points across. He didn't want to lie, and he didn't want to tell her why he reacted the way he did.

"Something is wrong," he said hesitantly, "I just don't want to talk about it."

"Now that's a better answer." Mary nodded. "Does it have anything to do with the new pastor and his wife?"

Walter inhaled. "Yes, I knew them both years ago at separate times. It was a shock to hear that they are together."

"Ah," Mary nodded. "I see. So what was wrong with them?"

"I can't talk about that." Walter sighed. "I really can't. Maybe they have changed."

"So you are withholding judgment until you can say if they are converted or not?"

"Something like that." Walter nodded. "Yes, definitely that."

"In the meantime, the elder's board wanted to know if you wanted to plan a party for them."

"No!" Walter snapped. "Most definitely not!"

Mary frowned. "This is interesting. You never miss a

chance to plan a party, Walter Wiley. How bad was it with those two? On a scale of one to ten with ten being the worst?"

Walter chuckled dryly, "Oh Mary, can I just go inside and join the rest of the elders?"

"They won't miss us, they are discussing the homework program to begin next week. it's basically the same old stuff, a new class was added to accommodate the volume of students we have for the sciences.

"Tell me how bad was it with the pastor and his wife or I will insist to the rest of the board that you plan his welcome party and then when you say no, I will insist that you tell us why."

"Blackmail, really?" Walter raised an eyebrow, "isn't that a sin too?"

"Don't think of it as blackmail," Mary cajoled, her eyes twinkled mischievously, "think of it as me wanting to help you. You look like you need to get this off your chest."

Walter scratched his chin. "Well for Axel I would give him a solid ten and Gia maybe an eight."

Mary nodded contemplatively. "Ten for the pastor, what on earth could he have done?"

"It was years ago," Walter sighed, "and I don't want to talk about it. It happened some time ago, the man could have made a one-eighty degree turn. I do not want to bring up something he must have asked forgiveness for and moved on from. And so I reserve my right to not speak about it for now."

"Okay, I'll accept that for now, but I am far from happy about you keeping this mammoth secret from the eldership. A ten is a big deal. Now I'll be imagining what it could be."

Mary contorted her face in disgust. "I hate this Walter. I hate what is happening to this church. It's like a revolving door these days. The pastors are passing through as if this is a pit stop. If it's not one problem, it's another."

Walter sighed. "They are human and fallible."

"I know they are human but why are they still so weak, back in my days we had some solid men of the cloth." Mary lamented. "Solid men. I think Christianity is dying."

"It is very much alive and probably still the same." Walter shrugged. "The old clerics just hid their sins better. Christianity is not dying; there will always be followers of Jesus Christ, our problems stem from people not being like him."

"You have a point," Mary said, "but I wish for once we could get a humble, God-fearing man. You know what, I'll plan the party, but I won't do anything fancy, just in case this new one doesn't stay. I don't want to waste my time. You know I was the party planner around here before you came and usurp me."

Walter smiled. "Sorry about that."

"I'll get Ivan to help me. You know he is living with me now?"

"I know." Walter nodded. Ivan was Mary's grandson, her favorite of what seemed like a million grandchildren. He had moved in with her because his parents had both gone back to school.

Renee, Elder Mary's daughter, went to do her doctor of laws degree and Vincent went to do some specialist degree in medicine to enhance his already thriving practice.

Ivan, their only child, had moved in with his grandmother and was quite happy to get a break from his overachieving parents.

"He is so unhappy now." Mary sighed. "He may have to repeat fourth form."

Walter grimaced. "Again?"

"Yes." Mary shook her head. "What can I say? He was

even failing Religious Studies. Pastor White was helping him with that, and he actually got a B. I was going to see if this new pastor could help. I try with him Walter, I really do. We read together, but it's as if that boy's brain is broken."

Walter stiffened when he heard about the new pastor helping out boys. He would never trust Axel around any boy; he didn't care if he was married to Gia now.

Walter cleared his throat and said cautiously. "Maybe you shouldn't have this new pastor tutoring Ivan privately. Why don't you have him join the homework program?"

Mary nodded. "I already have him enrolled in all the classes, every day of the week. What can I say? I am clutching at straws here. The boy will not be turning a man in high school, not under my watch."

Chapter Two

Walter drove home after the meeting. He couldn't shake the bad taste in his mouth, and he desperately needed to talk to someone, preferably one of his brothers. He sat in his car and looked at the other houses.

Preston's living room light was on. It was a year and a half since his marriage to Sheryl. She was due to give birth to their daughter any day now. It was so imminent they had the hospital bag packed and at the front door.

He couldn't disturb Preston or Sheryl now, nor did he want Pete to hear about what he went through with Axel. He didn't want to particularly relive it with Preston either.

He looked over at Jordan's place. He was probably entertaining. There were a couple of cars parked before his house which was the norm these days since Shawn had given birth to a baby girl six months ago, Courtney Mason Wiley.

Jackie, the doting grandmother, was a constant visitor at the house. She was probably there now. He wasn't going to bring up anything about his past ordeal with Jackie around.

Walter drummed his hand on the steering wheel. That left Guy his only single brother of the older set and Guy wasn't likely to be home, not on a weekday, not these days. Walter had jokingly told him to rent out his townhouse because he was hardly there.

Guy liked to stay at his farmhouse in the hills. And it was easy to see why. One had the tendency to forget that the place was a working farm and not an eco-resort.

The place was twenty-five acres of perfection in the St. Andrew hills. It took a while to get to the place but when you did you were treated to fabulous views of the rolling hills, a variety of birds to entertain a bird lover for months and a waterfall and river on the property that was big enough to raft on.

The farmhouse itself was sprawling and rustic. Guy recently had it built to take advantage of the views. Walter thought enviously of relaxing in the hammocks on Guy's long veranda. He leaned back in his car seat with a sigh.

Unfortunately, he couldn't do that, he was vice president of finance of Wiley Corp, Preston's second in command and he wasn't due for a vacation yet.

When it was time, he would be going to the hills, but for now, he was on his own with this latest momentous news. His other brothers were MIA.

Case was on a European tour. He hadn't even come home for the Christmas holidays, and Saint was out of the country. He was now away for a week and would be spending six months in the UK for training related to his security business.

Sandrene had gone with him for the duration. Their house was locked up. And so should Guy's.

He did a double take when he saw that Guy's kitchen light was on.

So Guy really was home! Walter joyfully got out of the car. He would have someone to dump his woes on for a while.

What a relief. One didn't have five brothers for nothing. He headed to Guy's house. It was beside his. He knocked on the door once, tried the door and then stood back trying to get a look into the kitchen. The blinds were drawn, and he couldn't see a thing. That was unusual for Guy when he was home. He usually left the front door unlocked and did his house to house visiting.

And then he heard fumbling, and the porch light came on, and the door swung open.

"Walter!" A vaguely familiar-looking woman stood at the door.

"Hey!" Walter said smiling confusedly at her. He hadn't known that Guy had company.

The lady grinned. "Don't tell me you don't recognize me."

"I don't." Walter frowned.

She laughed. "It's the hair, isn't it? I stopped perming it and went natural."

She twirled a lock of thick curly hair around her fingers.

"Or the lack of braces?" She flashed straight white teeth in a smile.

"Or the fact that I am not wearing my glasses." She batted her eyelashes at him, "I have in contacts. I would be blind without them otherwise and truth be told I am in a love hate relationship with them right now."

"Aisha Fire!" Walter whispered hoarsely. "The voice and the chattiness gave you away. Goodness, you look different."

"You got it!" Aisha squealed and moved from the door and hugged him.

She fitted right in his arms. Slim and shapely she looked up at him and laughed. "I told Guy. I said bet Walter doesn't recognize me."

"You still keep in touch with Guy?" Walter whispered still reeling in disbelief. This could not be Aisha Fire. The Aisha Fire he knew was Gia's ugly duckling cousin.

"What on earth are you doing here?" Walter asked still in disbelief.

Obviously, today was the day his past came to meet him three fold. First, he heard about Gia and Axel and now Gia's cousin, who had zoomed past ugly duckling status and was completely transformed into a swan.

He could not imagine that she would look this good in a million years. She was stunning.

She had the thin nose, high cheekbones and dusky complexion that was common with the Fire women and her hair was down, he could not recall seeing it down.

"Are you sure that you are Aisha Fire?" Walter asked again incredulously.

Aisha nodded and laughed. "Yup. I am sure. Want to see my passport?"

"Yes," Walter said seriously. "And then I want to hear all about why you are here tonight in my brother's house."

Aisha smiled. "Of course you would. Guy was gracious and kind to allow me to stay here for a while. He says he is hardly here and that there is plenty of room and it would be no problem. I just moved the last of my boxes to his spacious, fabulous guest room."

"That's true." Walter nodded. "He never told me you two still kept in touch."

"We do though, Walter William Wiley." Aisha laughed. "Remember how I would call you WWW dot?"

Walter smiled. "Yes."

"I have to run," Aisha looked at him regretfully. "I have a date. You remember Greg Green? I ran into him today at work. He dropped his sister off at school today, just when I was walking toward the staff room."

"Yes." Walter frowned. "I remember him quite well. How is he these days? I haven't seen him since his father sold the business and he disappeared from the radar."

"They have a bakery." Aisha grinned. "And he gave me a box of donuts. Absolutely divine. I am looking forward to our continued association."

"Be careful around Greg," Walter muttered. "He is not the most upstanding man in town, and he is a player."

"Thank you for the warning," Aisha said solemnly and winked at Walter, "but I am twenty-six. God told me I would marry someone this year. Suppose he is the one. Our meeting was probably divinely orchestrated."

Walter chuckled. "I've always envied your ability to hear God so clearly."

Aisha nodded solemnly. "I do hear him. I was praying about the whole being single thing, and I heard as plain as day a voice say this is your year to get married. Be patient."

Walter couldn't hide the skepticism from his voice. "I see."

"And it so happens that this year I got the job at the posh private school, Surrey Prep. Twice the pay. Half the students."

"And you met Greg out of the blue." Walter finished for Aisha doubtfully.

"That's right," Aisha nodded, "but I am not dumb enough to think that every man I'll meet this year is the one. I am waiting for God to point me in the right direction."

"That's smart," Walter said relieved. He wouldn't trust Greg as far as he could throw him, "Where are you going?"

"Cricket match at Sabina Park... Premier League. You know I love my cricket."

"Yes, I remember. We used to watch a lot of matches together in the student lounge."

Aisha grinned. "And cry when the Windies lost and sing rally round the West Indies at the top of our voices when they won."

Walter laughed. "You cried, I didn't."

"Come now, I remember differently." Aisha winked at him. "One day after a particularly tense match I saw tears at the corner of your eyes."

Walter laughed. "Rubbish."

"If you are up when I get back we can talk some more." Aisha offered. "It's really good to see you again, Walter."

Walter nodded and stepped back. "Yes, it is good to see you again, Aisha."

She gave him a jaunty little wave and headed back into the house.

Walter walked over to his place and headed to his courtyard patio. It wasn't exactly Guy's place in the hills, but it had its own secluded charm. He had Shawn design it so that he felt like he was in a resort. He even had a fountain out there and various seating areas to accommodate at least thirty persons because he did a lot of entertaining.

He figured he did it because he hated being alone with his own thoughts for long periods of time.

Tonight it was unavoidable. He went to one of the lounge chairs, loosened the two top buttons of his shirt and looked up into the clear night sky. Maybe tonight he needed to remember.

Chapter Three

Walter looked around the dorm room at Mount Faith. He didn't want to live on campus, but Preston had insisted, and now he had to share a room with a stranger. He sat on the bed that he had chosen and looked through the window. He was on the second floor of the three-story dorm called Austin House named after one of the founding father's of the school.

It was overcast. Dark, ominous looking clouds were slowly gathering in the east. It reflected how he felt inside. He was wound up so tight and felt so uneasy these past months that he had no idea if he would ever feel normal again.

He even thought that leaving Portland, leaving the house on Spring Street would have been the antidote to his misery but it was proving not to be. He still felt the same, except now he was missing his brothers on top of feeling like most of the life had been sucked out of him.

He should have seen a counselor. He should talk about this

with someone because he wasn't getting better.

He was now starting to have nightmares about Axel Parks pinning him down, and pressing his body against his. It had become so bad that he was even questioning his sexuality.

Was he gay? Why had Axel Parks tried something with him had he given off some invisible signal?

He closed his eyes wearily. Was something wrong with him? Tears welled up in his eyes, and he bid them not to fall.

This was not happening to him.

This was not happening to him.

He said the familiar mantra that usually worked to relax him for days at a time. It had worked when he heard that his mother was dead and she killed his father. It had worked when he heard that Fred had stolen all their money and they wouldn't have anywhere to live, it had worked until now.

Maybe it wasn't working now because he wasn't a kid anymore. He was seventeen years old, he would be eighteen in seven months. He couldn't be protected by childish mantras. Horrifying events did have an effect on him no matter if he willed it to or not.

If he were to be honest, he had no idea if he would recover from this, he still felt shell-shocked.

Maybe if it hadn't been Axel Parks of all the people in the world, he wouldn't be feeling this way. Axel had been his trusted friend, the person that he hung out with the most in the past year; he had spent more time with Axel than he did with his brothers.

And he had gotten no indication that he was even remotely like that. He had even confessed to Axel and no one else, not even Guy, who he usually told these things, that Mrs. Allen, his friend Ike's mother had propositioned him. She had seen him in the town and offered to drop him home.

He had only been just turned fifteen. It was the first day

of school, he had found it odd that Ike had not been with her, but he had taken the lift anyway. He listened while she made small talk—her husband was mean to her, and she just wanted love.

He had thought at the time how terrible her husband was because she was a very attractive woman. She looked like a picture that the vice principal had in her office of a beautiful dark-skinned woman in a dance pose with the title Ashanti Queen.

He had always thought Mrs. Allen was a bit like that woman and he had always admired that about her and then she had put her hand on his leg and squeezed it gently.

"This is between me and you, Walter. You are such a handsome young man, I can't imagine how fine you will be when you grow up."

Walter had grown increasingly alarmed when she had started to rub her hand along his leg.

He hadn't been repulsed, but he hadn't been attracted to her. He had felt a shaft of disappointment that she wasn't the Ashanti queen. Ashanti queens didn't rub boy's legs and tell them they were handsome.

She must have sensed his disillusionment because she stopped. She dropped him home and looked at him with displeasure.

"I know this is sudden, but you don't have to act like this. I'll pick you up tomorrow from school and we'll go somewhere private. You can relax then. It will be worth your while."

He had exited the car in alarm feeling a bit traumatized by the whole thing. He had avoided her after that if he saw her car in the town he actually ducked into a shop until she passed. If she came over to the school, he hid in classrooms.

He had even stopped talking to Ike. He didn't want to hear

anything about his mommy. The boy adored his mother and what was worse he didn't want to be invited to his birthday parties or anything that would bring him into contact with Mrs. Allen. He didn't even know her first name!

He had told Axel about it only because Axel had seen Mrs. Allen drop him home and had read his body language quite clearly.

Axel probably had filed it away for a later date when he planned his own assault on Walter. He should have known that something was different that day. Axel had been acting weird. He had asked him if he wanted to see a different African movie and he had eagerly said yes and then Axel had handed him a drink.

"Root beer," Axel had made it a point to announce, he sat beside Walter in the settee. "I know you boys don't drink."

Walter had taken a sip of the beer and it had tasted different. It smelled like it had alcohol and then he had taken another sip and looked over at Axel. "This is good."

"Drink it up." Axel had touched his cup to Walter's and then smiled at him.

"Let's watch the movie." Axel turned on the DVD with the remote.

Walter had started to feel woozy, and he was more than shocked when the opening credits of the movie showed a naked man and another naked man kissing.

He turned to look at Axel but he wasn't feeling too well, Axel was actually blurry and then he pushed his face close to Walter's.

"I love Jordan, you know that. I am in love with your brother, but I know he loves girls. So I don't stand a chance with him, but you are perfect. You don't have a girlfriend, you don't like women. You pushed away Mrs. Allen."

"You probably don't know that you like hanging with me

because you are in love with me. I am going to make this easier for you, Walter, and do what you want without the guilt."

And then Axel kissed him like he saw boys and girls do. He had never kissed a girl before, Walter had thought woozily. He had never found anyone he was even close to being tempted to kiss and then he couldn't remember anything else.

Walter snapped out of his reverie. As usual, when he thought about that evening, he felt dirty.

His first kiss was with Axel Parks, his youth pastor, and former friend. Thankfully, he couldn't remember most of it. How was he ever going to live this down?

There was a brief knock on the dorm room door, and then he heard it being opened with a key.

It would be the new roommate. Walter swiped his hand over his eyes, quickly glanced at the mirror to make sure that his eyes weren't red and then waited for his roommate to appear.

He walked in with his parents behind him.

"Hello, I am Greg Green." He walked over and shook Walter's hand enthusiastically. He looked a little goofy. He had on jeans and a pink sweater with a bear on the front. He was very fair skinned, his hair was wavy and cut in one of those mohawk styles and he had a tattoo of a bird on his neck.

Walter shook his hand and was introduced to his parents, Michael and Lydia Green—an interracial couple. The father was white, an obviously older gentleman and the mother was black. She reminded him a bit of Sharla.

Walter watched a little enviously as the Green family interacted. They were clearly close. The mother, Lydia cried before they left.

"Both of you take care of each other. I hope you will be

good friends."

Walter nodded, he hoped so. It would be in his best interest to be on good terms with his roommate.

"Thank God they are gone!" Greg said bouncing on the bed at the other side of the room. "I am free! Yipee!"

He pulled off the sweater unceremoniously and hunted in his suitcase for a much more manly looking black jacket.

"I had to wear this pink sweater," Greg said to Walter sheepishly, "my mother wanted me to, I didn't want to argue because this was my last day at home and she and I have been at it about the tattoo."

"Is it permanent?" Walter frowned.

"No." Greg grimaced, "I wish it were. I tested them with it and they almost had a heart attack. My dad was horrified at what the church folk would think. You know we own a distributing firm and my Dad is like a deacon at his church. Anglicans are very conservative."

Walter nodded. "I know and I agree with them. I don't like tattoos."

"Say what?" Greg raised an eyebrow in shock. "It is the thing now."

"I hate them." Walter shuddered, "I seriously hate them, that and body piercings."

"And I was thinking of getting my tongue done." Greg giggled. "And my ears too."

"It's your body," Walter grunted. "I won't be doing any of those things to myself."

They had identical furniture at both ends of the room and a fairly large space between them.

Walter hadn't unpacked either, so he moved his suitcases closer to his section; Greg had twice as many bags as he did.

"You don't like tats and piercings, but please say you like to party," Greg pleaded, "because I can't wait to party! My cousin used to come to this school, and he says they have the wackiest house parties around here. I need to get invited to some."

"Yes, I like to party," Walter nodded eagerly. He was thinking tame birthday parties and church functions not wild raves.

Greg rubbed his hands together with glee. "And the girls, man. Can't wait to meet the girls. I mean, while I was driving on the campus I saw girls, very pretty girls. They were walking in packs, brown ones, dark ones, and shapely ones. It's like a beauty pageant up here."

Walter chuckled. "I didn't see any girls."

"Are you blind man?" Greg asked with his mouth opened.

"No, Just took the back gate. There were no girls on that side of campus."

Greg laughed. "Well it doesn't matter, we will see a ton of them shortly. According to the schedule, the cafeteria opens in an hour. I am famished, and I want to meet pretty girls."

Walter shrugged. "I am not hungry, we own a supermarket, and I carried a load of snacks."

Greg shook his head. "No man, it doesn't matter. You are coming to the caf with me. It's our time to mingle. Get in on the ground with some of the hottest girls. At my old high school, they couldn't get enough of me. I bet they were all over you too."

Walter was about to protest that he wasn't much in the mood to party or pick up girls but when had he ever felt like picking up girls?

The question came back to haunt him. Why wasn't he as enthusiastic about girls like Greg was.

Was Axel right about him? Was he gay?

But he didn't like guys either. He knew that for a fact. He had felt repulsion when Axel kissed him, at least from what he could remember. He had felt just as disgusted when Mrs. Allen had propositioned him.

Through the years he had not found anybody attractive nor did he have the faintest desire to be bouncing on his bed and looking forward to seeing girls like Greg.

Maybe he was asexual. He had never stopped to consider that. In a sexualized world he was an anomaly. He was neither attracted to males nor females. One thing was for sure he wasn't like anybody else his age. All his brothers were different. Even his little brother Case had a girlfriend.

****

The semester continued much the same way it began. Greg literally acted like a child in a candy shop. Even Walter had to admit there was an infusion of pretty girls at Mount Faith University.

They were such a common sighting that he had no idea why Greg was still so excited about seeing them. In the space of four and a half months Greg had run through several girlfriends it was getting harder to keep track of their names.

Walter honestly doubted that Greg was spending any meaningful time in classes. He always seemed to be taking one or the other of his little harem to breakfast, lunch or supper. He was always making up or breaking up with them, and Walter was expected to be the sounding board for why one of his temporary relationships went south.

It was a probably a good thing that Greg was so caught up in his own little girl world that he didn't realize that Walter was not exactly happy. He still had difficulty sleeping at nights. His only antidote was spending all of his nights in the gym.

After a hard session, his body had no recourse but to

collapse in exhaustion. His muscles were getting stronger and thicker, but his mind was still broken. He wished he could just forget about what happened with Axel.

He wished that the memories could just dry up and die. He was seriously envious of people with amnesia.

His only bright note were classes, they were quite easy. He was beginning to think that university was overhyped, or maybe his business classes were just too easy. After all, he already had the experience of helping to run a business.

He had the knowledge of the inner workings of a fairly complicated business, so introductory courses were like learning ABC's all over again.

He was contemplating taking on even more business courses next semester when Greg burst into the room excitedly.

"I scored! I met the prettiest, and I do mean the prettiest girl yet. I love her, man. She is the one and this is true love."

Walter was slowly getting into bed for a much-needed rest. His muscles were screaming, he had literally tortured himself at the gym.

"Congrats," he groaned.

"She is fire!" Greg stood in the middle of the room and curved his hands against his chest and hips imitating a womanly figure, "literally fire."

"Good for her, may she forever burn bright." Walter settled down in the bed with a long drawn out sigh. He would sleep like a baby tonight.

"I mean it. Her name is Gia Fire," Greg said, "I literally feel hot just thinking about her. Her father's family are from Ethiopia and get this, Ethiopians don't have surnames like we do."

"They don't?" Walter closed his eyes wearily even his eyelids seemed as if they were in pain.

"No. They just have one name. Isn't that cool? When her father and her aunts and uncles moved to this side of the world, they took their father's first name as a surname. So Gia's grandfather was named Fire."

"That's amazing," Walter whispered. He was sure that the information was amazing, but he was just not feeling enthusiastic about anything but sleep.

"Yes, it is super cool." Greg was salivating. "I asked her on a date Saturday night. I was thinking something tame like the Student Center but get this, Gia knows of an off-campus house party!

"I am telling you, Walter, the girl knows everybody. Anyway, she said yes to the date but on one condition—we have to take her annoying cousin along. The cousin is younger and apparently some math prodigy, and they are temporary roommates. Gia doesn't want her to rat on her, so she has to come."

"Good for you," Walter murmured. He was barely listening to Greg. His brain was like liquid mush.

"And good for you too," Greg said," because you are Aisha's date."

Walter was too tired to even respond.

Chapter Four

Walter went with Greg to the house party out of sheer defeat. Greg would not take no for an answer and he had nagged Walter into submission. Besides, there was nothing that he was interested in doing that night. He couldn't go to the gym, he needed a rest day for his overworked muscles to recuperate and he was not terribly interested in hanging out at the recreation center at the student lounge building.

So he was in with Greg, reluctantly. He had been hoping for rain but the night was almost perfect. Not too cold, not warm with clear skies and a canopy of stars. He spotted the big dipper and then from there the north star.

He told Greg who looked at him as if he had walked out of Nerdsville.

"I don't want to talk about stars," Greg said dismissively, "I want to talk about Fire. Gia Fire. Wait until you see this girl, Walter, you will wish you were me."

The girl's dorm was a half a mile from theirs. True to his

word, Greg kept up a running commentary about Gia. Greg was so enamored he never ran out of superlatives to describe her.

Walter was skeptical about Gia until he saw her for himself. She was standing on the porch of the dorm and instantly he knew it was her. She was dressed in black latex pants and an eye-wateringly tight sheer red blouse, and she didn't have on a bra.

He could see her breasts printed out in the blouse quite clearly. She shrugged on a jacket when they came nearer. That was when Greg remembered to breathe.

Gia was tall and slim, yet curvy and she was indeed pretty when he remembered to look on her face and not her chest.

She had a smooth mocha complexion, thick pillow soft lips which were painted a bright red to match her blouse and long thick hair that fell at her waist. She was the type of girl you saw in movies.

Walter found himself staring at her far longer than was polite; she had an unreal quality about her. He could see why Greg was so smitten.

Her friend Aisha was not as attention grabbing though. He had the cynical thought that that was why she was chosen to be Gia's friend and then he remembered that they were relatives.

"Aisha is my cousin," Gia said after they were introduced.

Aisha smiled at him shyly. She had in thick braces and wore horn-rimmed glasses. She was the kind of person that one would automatically peg as a stereotypical nerd.

"I love your name, it is very pretty." Walter smiled at her. "Reminds me of a song I played on repeat in high school."

"Really?" Aisha grinned at him, and he could see glimmers of a very good-looking girl behind the smile.

They decided to walk the two miles to the party, which was

at one of the mansions on the outskirts of the campus.

Aisha turned out to be quite entertaining and talkative. "You are gorgeous Walter!"

"Thank you." Walter grinned. Aisha was frank and bubbly and reminded him a little bit of Shawn. The closest person he had as a sister.

"I mean it," Aisha whispered, "I think the Queen is regretting choosing the brainless one for her date and sticking me with you."

"I heard that." Gia spun around.

"Me too," Greg said looking wounded, "I am not brainless."

"Well good for you," Aisha said saucily, "your hearing is impeccable Queen G, why don't you concentrate on your own date."

"Stop calling me Queen G in that snarky tone," Gia growled. "I have no idea why I even associate with you. You are annoying."

"Oh, I was supposed to use a subservient tone, wasn't I?" Aisha grinned. "We are in Jamaica, the royal house of Solomon was dissolved in 1974, subservience is not gonna happen, Queenie."

Gia started walking faster, and Greg started trotting to catch up with her.

"What's that about?" Walter asked. The dynamics between the cousins was fascinating, and he was curious about the royalty angle.

"Oh, it's nothing." Aisha grinned. "I overheard Queen G on the phone with some gullible admirer telling them that her mother is from the royal House of Solomon."

"Which I am" Gia stopped walking, put her hands on her hips and glared at Aisha. "You are so jealous, Aisha."

"Me! Jealous, of you!" Aisha groaned. "You wish."

"Let's get this straight," Gia said viciously. "I am not afraid to tell people of my family history. My mother can track her lineage from the King of Solomon and the Queen of Sheba. "

"Solomon in the Bible?" Greg whispered, "that's way cool."

"My father married my mother just before members of the royal family was either chased out of Ethiopia or jailed in the seventies. They moved to Jamaica when they were pretty young."

Gia flipped her hair over her shoulder and looked at Walter. "You must have heard of him, Bishop Fire from the House of Fire. He is popular on cable channels."

Walter shook his head. "I haven't."

"Well you'll check him out now that you know me," Gia said flippantly. "My Dad is a fire and brimstone chewing, the Lord is going to get you kind of preacher. He's crazy I tell you, but people love him. Apparently, they love hearing about how angry God is and how he is going to punish them for their various sins. I am so used to it now, I am tired. I have fire and brimstone fatigue. Seventeen years of it…"

Greg laughed. "We don't usually preach that kind of thing at our church, righteousness by fear doesn't work long term. It might get people in, but it doesn't keep them. God is love."

"But he is also a judge," Walter said, "I guess there has to be a balance about how we present him to people. There should be balance in everything."

Gia looked at him and smiled. "A philosophical response."

They ditched the royal family topic when they were halfway to the party.

Gia took over the conversation altogether and had succeeded in cowing Aisha into silence.

She started talking about her past escapades sneaking out of her house in Montego Bay and going to street dances.

"It was wild," she grinned, "and my dad was clueless.

Some of my party friends are up here in this shutdown boring place, and we are going to have fun. My dad thought he was reining me in, but I am just about to bust loose."

Aisha looked at Walter and rolled her eyes. "Unfortunately, I am stuck with this party queen until I can get another room. I just hope Lady Gia from the Royal House of Solomon keeps her grades up."

"Which I will," Gia said flippantly. "Pretty girls don't have to work as hard.

"And you are the prettiest of them all," devotion dripped from Greg's voice. "Ethiopian girls are the most beautiful women in the world."

"That's right." Gia shrugged, "I am a direct descendant of the Queen of Sheba. Some of her beauty has rubbed off."

"Queen G at it again," Aisha whispered under her breath, only Walter could hear and he chuckled quietly.

Gia was obviously not above highlighting her own attributes. It was a turnoff.

Sometime during the night, Walter concluded that she was practically a wild child. She didn't act like somebody coming out of a Christian household. If he hadn't heard that her father was Bishop Fire, he would have concluded that she grew up in the middle of a dancehall. She knew all the latest tunes. She chugged alcohol like a hardened drinker, and she danced like a pro.

Greg was with her wholeheartedly, the wide-eyed wonder look that he had when they had just entered the house, and the pool area was replaced by a smug smile as he and Gia contorted themselves around each other on the dance floor.

Walter found all of it slightly dull, the music was jarring, the taste of liquor reminded him of the incident with Axel, and the party games seemed a bit juvenile. He couldn't relax enough to be as carefree and lighthearted as his peers.

Even Aisha who had seemed to be a bit more conventional had melted into the crowd and was mingling.

Walter left the house. It was not his scene. He was not in the right frame of mind for something like this. He walked back to the dorm alone.

****

Things got easier. He stopped having frequent nightmares and he slept through the night without killing himself at the gym. He did two summer sessions packing in more credits than was necessary.

He moved off dorm for the summer and was living in a very reasonably priced apartment that was teeming with Mount Faith students.

He was surprised to see that Gia Fire was his neighbor. He had not thought of her much since the night of the party. She and Greg had been involved in a very short romance, which had not ended well. Gia had dumped him and called him boring.

Greg had cried as if his world was ending. It was so bad he had not cared that the whole dorm knew that his heart was broken.

"She grabbed my heart from my chest and squeezed it in her perfect hands," he declared.

By week three Greg had seemingly moved on and was calling her some choice names and declaring that he wished he had never met her.

When Walter moved into his new digs, Gia was moving into hers, she waved to him enthusiastically.

"Walter! How are ya?"

"Good." Walter couldn't help feeling a little star struck when he saw her, but he covered it with a casual attitude.

"How are you?"

"Great!" Gia chuckled. "I got my mom to convince my dad that I could live off campus since I am now eighteen. I see your parents let you out too."

"I don't have parents." Walter shrugged. "This move is purely financial prudence. My older brother thought that living on dorm for the summer was too expensive."

"Well, you have to convince him to let you stay off." Gia made a face. "The dorm situation is too restrictive. Say, you want to go to a house party tonight?"

"No thanks. Not my kind of thing."

"Let me guess, you are trying to save face because you flunked the semester and that is why you are doing summer?" Gia asked sympathetically. "That must suck."

"No, I did well, you are way off the mark." Walter smiled. "I just want to hurry this school experience along."

"Me too." Gia grinned. "Apparently I can party and still make good grades. I think I am a genius or something. I just have to look at something once, and I can remember whole blocks of text. I can summon it just like that." Gia snapped her fingers.

"Lucky you," Walter murmured enviously.

"Yes," Gia opened her door and then spun around and looked at him. "You know, you are the first guy I have ever told about my photographic memory, and you didn't say something trite like beauty and brains all in one package."

Walter shrugged. "I don't do trite. But that is a great ability you have there. If I had a photographic memory the things I would do. If you'll excuse me, I have some more boxes to get from the driveway."

"Wait," Gia frowned, "what did Greg tell you about us?"

"Nothing much, he did say he wished he had never met you and he called you a bunch of unsavory names." Walter raised an eyebrow. "Why?"

"I was..." Gia frowned, "I am not used to men treating me so casually. You aren't even making an effort to flirt with me. Everybody likes me. Everybody thinks I am pretty."

Walter laughed at her expression; she knew how to pout prettily. "You are pretty. I just don't flirt."

He left Gia standing at his door and went to get his boxes. "You need help to unpack?"

"Sure, why not," Walter said, "I didn't peg you as the helping me to unpack kind of girl."

"I didn't know I was either," Gia grimaced. "I must be short-circuiting."

Walter laughed.

He laughed because he quickly realized two things about Gia. She was so used to getting fawned over that his cool laid back attitude toward her was a novelty, and two if he treated her just as a friend she would become obsessed with them being more.

****

His brothers minus Jordan came to visit him for his birthday in August. Jordan was in the States for Shawn's graduation. Pastor Tate and his family drove with them because Preston wanted to deliver his car. Preston was upgrading to a new vehicle and Walter would get his mother's old BMW.

They went to the Two Hearts Villa in Negril for the weekend, which was run by Shawn's aunt Ava. They had a whale of a time.

Ava made sure that the boys had fun. Lady Adalynn cornered him after games night when everybody had trudged off to bed.

"Hey Walter, just a word." She looked at him and smiled,

but he could see the concern at the back of her eyes. "How are you doing these days?"

"Good," Walter said uncomfortably. He knew what she was asking about and he was not in the mood to discuss Axel and how he was coping in the aftermath.

"You know," Adalynn said conversationally, "I don't expect you to be over what happened and I know you won't talk to anybody about what you are feeling but I just want you to know, you are in my prayers every single day. I hope one day you will be willing to confide in somebody about it."

Walter nodded. "Okay."

Adalynn sighed. "I hate that you think you have to do this alone."

"I am fine." Walter almost scowled. They had an enjoyable evening, and this lady was coming to him with the dark things that he was busy burying.

"Okay," Adalynn stood up. "Just so you know, time heals, Walter. Remember that when things get too dark."

They went back to Portland the day after, but Guy stayed behind to spend a week with him.

Walter hoped it would convince Guy to attend Mount Faith since it was close to home but Guy wasn't particularly interested in Mount Faith. Uncle Micky had started leaning more and more on him as his right-hand man and Guy would not leave the old man hanging.

Guy's one fascination that week seemed to be Gia.

When he first saw her, he had shaken his head and looked out the window of the apartment again.

"Tell me she is real," Guy whispered hoarsely.

"She is real." Walter was curiously not that interested in her, he must have gotten used to her looks.

"And she lives beside you?" Guy asked. "How do you manage every day knowing she is breathing right next to you. Behind these walls."

Guy put his ear to the wall and tried hugging it with great exaggeration.

Walter laughed. "Want me to introduce you to her?"

"Yes! Can you do it now?" Guy said jumping up and down like an excited puppy.

Walter called Gia on his cell phone, and Gia came almost instantly.

She usually rushed to come over when he called. Walter found it funny. The girl that everybody seemed to be going bonkers over would do anything he said. It was kind of empowering.

Guy instantly went into shy mode when she came over and started tripping over his own speech. Gia loved it.

"He is cute, very nice curly hair," Gia said dismissively and then turned to Walter her eyes alight with excitement. "I see you got a car, Walter."

"Yes," Walter nodded. "I got a car."

"You know what that means, Gia clapped her hands in glee, we can go to Negril for Spring Break, Carnival in Kingston, street dances, I've never been to an honest to goodness one. I hear they have some really good ones in Santa Cruz.

Guy opened his eyes wider and wider in shock as Gia kept talking and Walter chuckled.

"No Gia. For the umpteenth time, I am not into that kind of lifestyle."

"We'll see," Gia said blowing him a kiss and exiting the apartment.

"She is trouble," Guy said in disappointment when she left the apartment. "She is the kind of girl that mothers warn their boys to steer clear of. This sucks. She would have made a very pretty girlfriend for you."

Walter shrugged. "I don't like her like that."

"I see." Guy sat down on the settee across from Walter and frowned. "You should make an effort to like her."

"Why?" Walter widened his eyes.

"Just because..." Guy cleared his throat, "she can distract you. I know you haven't been the same since the thing..."

"Since Axel tried to rape me," Walter said helpfully.

"Since that," Guy squirmed in the seat. "I read where people who were molested when they were young by the same sex could become you know, gay molesters too."

Walter groaned out loud. "I am not gay, and I wasn't actually molested. I came close to being molested, and it does bother me because I can remember him kissing me and I had nightmares of the whole thing, but I may be getting better. It doesn't hurt as much anymore."

Guy exhaled and sat back on the settee. "Thank God for that. But I don't understand you have never really liked girls even before that."

"Maybe it will kick in one day," Walter shrugged, "And maybe not. Maybe I am the asexual brother. There are a few people in the world like that you know?"

"What a sorrowful state to be in when you live beside beautiful bodacious bad Gia," Guy said dreamily. "And she seems to like you."

"Maybe because I don't like her," Walter said, "amazing how that works, huh?"

Chapter Five

His second year of university was what Walter would call his busiest year. He packed his semester with so many classes he hardly saw his apartment or Gia. It wasn't until it was close to December that he realized that she was trying to get his attention.

Gia confronted him when he was on his way to Events Management class. It was one of those pesky electives in the bundle of courses that came under the creative umbrella. The school required that he chose one from that bundle to make him a well-rounded individual. He chose Events Management because it sounded fun, at least more fun than Creative Writing or Art Expressions.

The class had nothing to do with finance or his goal to be vice president of finance for Wiley Incorporated, and it wasn't even really a class as such. His teacher, Justine Figueroa, was an actual event planner and had so much going on that she was using her students as cheap labor.

Walter had never had so much fun in his entire life. The Christmas season was chock-full of appointments for Miss Figueroa and her team; they had faculty parties, birthday parties, corporate events, and her cousin's wedding.

The twelve of them in the class were given a grab bag, from which they had to choose an event to plan and organize with an employee from Justine's company, *We Figueroa it Out*.

He had chosen her cousin's wedding. And he realized why he was the envy of the class. Planning weddings was complicated and his client Jessica was dingbat crazy. She inserted herself in the planning process and constantly made changes to her Christmas themed wedding. She changed so much Walter was never sure what was next.

They only had six weeks to work with, and they had a meeting at the venue.

"Walter you are so busy these days," Gia accused him, "Where ya going?"

He locked his door and turned to Gia. "I am going to the plantation house at Liberty Estates, they have a garden restaurant there."

"Can I come with you?" Gia pouted, "I am bored."

"I am going on business." Walter doubted that planning weddings would be an exciting thing for Gia. "We are planning a wedding. Liberty Estates is going to be the venue."

"Events Management class?" Gia raised an eyebrow. "I hear people talking about that course. I can come along and help."

"Okay." Walter shrugged. "You can't wear that though."

He pointed to her very short, very tight shorts and the low cut peasant blouse she was wearing.

"Oh, sure I'll change. Don't leave me, I'll be quick," Gia said heading into the apartment. She returned pretty quickly in jeans and a modest t-shirt which was surprising, Gia didn't do modesty very well.

He was going to use her dress as an excuse not to take her with him, but here she was looking like a regular person. She had even scraped back her long hair in a low ponytail and was make up free.

Usually, she had on inches of the stuff even though she didn't need it.

Walter was of two minds, should he take her to the meeting or would it be unprofessional?

He needn't have worried. Jessica took to Gia like they were long lost friends and they hashed out more details than he and Regina had done in three weeks.

When they were finished, they hung out at the student center and ate ice cream.

"You are looking really good, Walter." Gia raked her eyes over his biceps. "What do you do, sleep in the gym?"

"No," Walter shrugged. "I have late classes, and then I go to the gym and get the last hour before it closes, and then I shower and go to the library, do my assignments or group work..."

"Boring." Gia interrupted him with an exaggerated a yawn. "You should make some time on the weekends to party."

"No thanks, I go to church," Walter said, "I like going."

Gia made a face. "Church, blech! I used to go every day. When your father is Bishop Fire from the House of Fire, every day something was happening.

We had two services on Sundays. Mondays we had homework clinic for the younger people who were struggling in school. Tuesdays there was Pilates, my mother still teaches that. Wednesdays there was fasting and prayer meeting and a load of other stuff. Thursdays there was praise dance class. Fridays there was young people forum. Saturdays there were two church services again."

Walter chuckled. "So you guys had services on Saturdays and Sundays?"

"Yup. Double the offering." Gia smirked. "My dad had it all covered for the first day or seventh-day attendees, and I had to attend them both. It was crazy. You remember the first night when we were on the way to the house party, and you mentioned God being balanced."

"Yes," Walter nodded.

"I liked that," Gia snorted. "I wish my Daddy would be more like the Lord in that respect. If you kill somebody with something and don't give them room to breathe what do you expect?"

"Rebellion?" Walter raised an eyebrow at her.

"That's right," Gia smirked. "Rebellion. You should try it out."

"No," Walter said unconvincingly, he was contemplating his life though. Was this all there was? He would come to school, get outstanding grades, go back to Portland and move into the family business—home, work, gym and church for the rest of his life. He was just eighteen, and it sounded like a death sentence.

Gia looked at him knowingly. "You have to live, Walter, and this is the age to do it. You only live once, and these are your prime years. You need to try a cigar, drink some cognac, have unfettered wild sex."

Walter looked at Gia in shock. "You didn't just go there."

"We don't have to be in a relationship to do it." Gia snorted, "you are so uptight it's amazing. Can I tell you, Walter, I have never met a boy like you. Never. You are going to have to tell me, why you are so boringly conservative. You are still a virgin aren't you?"

Walter sighed. "That's none of your business."

"Oh, it is. I am going to pop your cherry." Gia clapped her hands in glee, "and you are going to like it. You are going to get hooked on me. I am that good."

She leaned in closer to Walter. He could feel the tendrils from her hair and smell her sweet almost fruity perfume. "You are fortunate to meet me in university Walter, I am as freaky as they come. You will no longer be the country bumpkin with the busy schedule when I am done with you. You will be like putty in my hands."

And then she placed her hands over the crotch of his pants and squeezed him playfully, all the while licking her lips.

Walter looked at her and swallowed. He had the strangest feeling when he looked into her dark brown eyes that he was looking into pools of temptation itself. The Bible text 'flee from the devil and he will flee from you' just popped into his head unexpectedly.

"That will never happen," he said, but his voice was weak.

"I will make you love me," Gia said smiling at him wickedly. "I am confident of it. Solomon didn't stand a chance against the queen of Sheba, you won't stand a chance against me."

Walter realized two things at that moment, Gia was the devil, and he wasn't asexual after all.

Chapter Six

One year and one month of Gia Fire, changed Walter significantly. She completely stripped him of his inhibitions. She took partying to another level and sexually had no restraints.

She boasted that she tried everything at least once. He usually tried to accommodate her thirst for adventure. They made a sex tape, produced and directed by Gia with him in bondage costume acting as her slave.

Gia wanted it for her own personal enjoyment she said. He just wanted to please her. He had become hooked on Gia by the year was over. He didn't know if he loved her or he was just obsessed.

She had him smoking marijuana, drinking copious bottles of Hennessy. He was a mess, and his brothers were concerned.

He wasn't keeping up with classes as much anymore, and he sacrificed gym time for parties. Every night was a street dance or a house party. Gia dragged him to an orgy that he remembered very little about because he was too stoned. He wanted it to stay that way.

His brief visits home during the Gia period of his life were very uncomfortable. His grades were slipping. His brothers were overly concerned about his lifestyle. He found his brothers' concern annoying, and he just did not care.

They weren't really living, were they? They were jealous that he had his freedom and he was doing precisely what boys his age did.

Preston threatened to stop paying for his tuition, but he ended up changing his mind after Jordan intervened.

He overheard them arguing about him one weekend after he returned home.

Preston was hopping mad, he was pacing the room and practically growling.

"Walter is smoking marijuana and drinking and partying like a fool. He is wasting the money I give him on frivolous things! How can he be a financial controller when he is spending like a maniac?

"He has no sense of what it is like to be fiscally responsible. Does he have any idea the way I have to work hard to keep this business afloat so that he can have a better education?

"I don't have a life because I want him to have one and this is how that ungrateful beast rewards me? By acting like some kind of playboy at one of the most expensive universities in Jamaica. I shouldn't have given him the car! My God, the boy is going to break me!"

"Calm down a moment and think about this," Jordan said gently, "his grades are still good."

"B's!" Preston hissed. "Walter is a straight A student. Nothing messes with that. Our mother ups and kills our father and your mother and Monique, but Walter still got A's. He was almost raped by Axel, but he still got A's. But this girl, what's her name? I am too angry to remember her name!"

"Gia Fire," Jordan supplied the name dutifully.

"She is leading him astray. She is evil incarnate." Preston hissed. "How can she be Bishop Fire's child. I mean, have you heard the man? He knows what he is talking about. How can he have the daughter of Jezebel? My sources at Mount Faith say that she is up for anything.

"I am going to have Walter take an STD test—for everything. That girl is the village bike. I heard that she has been actively involved with questionable men since she was barely fourteen.

"I am not sending him back to Mount Faith. Oh no, never again!"

"He has two semesters left plus the summer," Jordan said, "let him finish. He is twenty years old he is going to have to make up his mind about Gia by himself. His common sense will kick in eventually."

"I don't know," Preston said shaking his head. "I mean, I don't know if Walter has any common sense anymore, drugs has a tendency to kill common sense. You forget that he is a druggie. My God, my brother is taking drugs!"

Walter listened to them resentfully. He wondered who died and made Preston Wiley his boss. He felt like going into the room where Preston was thrashing him and just scream profanities in his holier than thou face.

How dare Preston declare that he had no common sense? He was just average for a man his age. How dare Preston talk about him like that?

He went to his room instead and tried to calm down, but he found that he couldn't. He needed something to take the edge off. Just a tiny draw from a spliff.

He got up and started pacing. If Preston came into the

room and said anything wrong about him or about Gia, he would deck him. He was bigger in body than Preston or even Jordan.

All his hours at the gym had bulked him up significantly. He could take on both Preston and Jordan and beat them into a pulp. Rage coursed through him out of nowhere, he was almost light-headed with it.

His head pounded in an alarming pulsing way, he clenched and unclenched his fists. Anybody coming through the door to confront him was going to get it.

And then he heard a knock.

"Come in!" he growled, all his pent-up hostility echoed through the two words.

Just say something—anything, his head, and his uneven emotions were egging him on.

But it was Jordan who came through the door; his expression was not one of accusation.

Walter felt somehow deflated. He had wanted Preston. He had wanted him to open his prissy mouth and say bad stuff against him so that he could rearrange it for him.

Jordan looked at him without speaking; he had compassion in his eyes and a kind of calming quality about him that immediately knocked off most of Walter's anger.

He folded his arms and leaned on the wall and looked him over.

"Let's go down to Otis' father's gym," Jordan said when he finally spoke. "Come on, let's get it all out on a punching bag."

Walter swallowed.

"Come on," Jordan headed to the door. "After that, we talk, okay? Just talk baby brother, no judgment. Just talk."

****

He did another summer school, this time not because he had any solid goals in mind but because Gia was doing the summer too. He spent most of his time at her apartment instead of classes, which was not a good idea; summer classes were on hyper speed. If you missed one, you missed the equivalent of a week in the regular semester. Gia had no problems skipping the occasional class, she had a photographic memory which was amazingly unaffected by her heavy partying lifestyle.

It was in the second summer session that things came to a head. She had been feeling distant lately, for most of July she had inexplicably ignored him. He was surprised when she had knocked on his door earlier and practically dragged him into her apartment to have sex.

Gia was looking at him now almost dispassionately. "I want to know all your private thoughts."

"My private thoughts?" Walter frowned. "Why?"

"Because...I want to know."

"Like what?" Walter was bewildered. She was acting weird. They usually spoke about her private thoughts. Anything outside of her thoughts was deemed uninteresting.

"First kiss?" She was making swirling shapes with her fingers on his belly.

"My first kiss?" Walter groaned, "unfortunately was with a man and I have no real recollection of it."

Gia was intrigued. She looked at him wide-eyed. "Really, tell me."

And he did. He was careful not to call Axel's name or give details that would identify him. He told her how confused and messed up he was after being assaulted—Gia nodded in understanding.

"You poor baby." Gia purred.

"I actually thought I might be gay or something. I didn't

like anyone, I was worried, and then I met you, and we became intimate, and I think, not think, I know that I love you Gia. I want us to be together forever."

Gia nodded smugly. "You love me?"

"Yes," Walter said earnestly." I think I really do. You've been distant these last couple of weeks, and I had the strangest thought that we were growing apart and I was literally panicking."

Gia got up from the bed unhurriedly and crossed her arms under her breasts and gave him a haughty smile. "Walter, have you lost your mind?"

Walter looked at her in confusion. "No, I am dead serious."

Gia laughed scornfully. "Get out of my apartment."

"What?" Walter was naked in bed. He got up slowly and looked at her, "Why?"

"Because you said I love you, ergo I conquered you," Gia said self-satisfaction dripping from her tongue. "I made you love me. Remember, you said I couldn't, but now you know I can. It was a challenge. Now game over."

Walter opened his mouth like a dying fish on a hook. "Gia, come on."

"Don't beg," Gia sneered, "please, whatever this was has run its course. It was a wild ride after you got over your shyness. I turned you into a real man, mission accomplished!"

"I can't believe this," Walter whispered. "This is not happening. I must be high and hallucinating."

"No, you are not hallucinating but that ecstasy pill surely made you chatty, and suddenly want to unpack your emotions on me." Gia pulled on a short nightgown that barely skimmed her thighs. "You said you thought you were gay. I helped you with that."

"I didn't say that." Walter frowned. "You are twisting what I said."

Gia fanned him off and pulled a cigar out of her side drawer. "You said you love me. I am having none of that. I don't want a lovesick boyfriend. I need bad Walter, I want hardcore. You are neither of those things. I thought I could shape you into that because you have the looks, but you don't quite have the attitude.

"There is always a little goody two shoes little boy lurking underneath that handsome face. I am bored. Besides I want to see other people. Other men. One year is more than enough for me to be monogamous."

Walter looked at Gia's as she lit her cigar and created smoke rings. He felt a shaft of pain in his chest.

He suddenly felt like crying.

"We are neighbors so I hope we can still be friends. Bye Walter." She blew a chain of smoke in his face and practically pushed him out of her apartment half naked.

"Gia come on. I didn't mean it. I didn't mean that I love you." He squealed in the corridor.

"Oh please," Gia snorted dismissively, "I know you love me now, you can't unsay it, you can't pretend indifference."

Walter pulled his keys out of his pants pocket and entered his apartment confusion and puzzlement enshrouding him in a cloud.

He had thought that they were getting on swimmingly. He had thought that they had the potential for something even better.

He had been living in an ecstasy land with the pills that Gia said would increase their enjoyment of each other.

He went into the bathroom, turned on the light and stared at himself in the mirror. She had used him and discarded him. All this time, one year and one month, Gia had just wanted him to say I love you so that she could kick him out of her life. She was interested in conquering him because of his initial indifference.

She had chosen him because he was conservative and uptight, she thought she would ruin him and she did. The woman was sick.

She had him hooked on a variety of prescription drugs and marijuana and alcohol and sex with her.

He stripped and stood in the shower with the cold water poring over his head. It was the cold and stiffness in his limbs that eventually registered and forced him out of the shower.

But it was desperation and a sense of deep, unsettling loneliness that had him calling Jordan.

He didn't even know that it was one in the morning. He called Jordan, and he had a long crying jag that must have taken Jordan by surprise.

Jordan was in Kingston, working. He knew he hung up after Jordan told him not to worry he'll be there by morning.

He fell asleep on the bathroom floor and was awakened by the door buzzer. It took him nearly twenty minutes to shuffle to the door. He looked at the clock, it was seven o'clock in the morning. He had a pounding headache, and he knew he looked like hell warmed up.

Jordan and Preston were on his doorstep, both of them looking almost as haggard as he was.

He let them in without a word and headed straight to the bed and covered his head with the sheet.

Sometime later that day his brothers arranged his life without much protest from him. Preston organized for him to spend a week at the Mount Faith Psych Center.

Admittance was free for students.

Jordan packed his clothes, and they drove him to the center across from campus. He finally saw a psychotherapist, and he had to admit it felt good unburdening all of his issues on somebody who listened without judging.

He ran through his messed up childhood, his tendency to go mute and shut down, the fact that deep down he still missed his mother. He knew he shouldn't, she was a monster who did very bad things but he had loved her, and he still did. He never stopped and he couldn't discuss it with his brothers.

The psychotherapist quickly summed up that he had trust issues, abandonment issues, control issues, and parenting issues. His list of issues was long enough to fill a year's subscription of Psychology Today.

Added to his myriad of emotional and mental issues, they had him on an outpatient detox program for six months.

He moved back on dorm, went back to church and started hitting the gym hard again. However, recovery for him was not an easy, seamless journey.

He still saw Gia on campus and she was still Gia. Still pretty, still with her entourage of sycophantic friends and panting men eagerly waiting for her to date them.

He felt a pang of...he couldn't describe it. Seeing Gia filled him with so many emotions and he had no idea how to classify them.

She was the girl who broke him, fortunately not completely. There were still pieces of him that were healing.

He headed in the other direction if he saw her approaching; he was treating her like what she was, poisonous.

He was on his way out of the student center when he passed Greg going in.

"Hey man," Greg greeted him enthusiastically. "I haven't seen you in a long while. What's up?"

"I am good." Walter nodded. "Lots of stuff to do. One year to go until graduation."

"Yeah, can't wait," Greg grinned. "You living back on campus now? Why man?"

"Because it is better for me." Walter sighed, "I went a little wild for a while."

"Gia will do that to you," Greg sighed, "apparently, I wasn't as wild as you. Have you heard who she is dating now?"

"I don't know anything about Gia," Walter said dismissively, "and I wouldn't care."

"You sure about that?" Greg grinned, "cause she left her phone in Economics class and I found it. I intended to give it back to her but I know she is always taking selfies, and I wanted to see what she was up to."

"Really Greg, I don't care."

"She had pictures," Greg ignored him, "she had lots of pictures. A couple naked ones, I had to copy her picture and video files. Unfortunately, while I was looking through I found that she had a couple of juicy videos. I have never found a juicier list of videos. That girl really gets around, doesn't she? Mostly parties and fully clothed dancing and stuff but really the stuff I saw would make Bishop Fire have paroxysms. I even saw one with you, that one was an eye-opener. You always seemed so old-fashioned, I had no idea you were a freak under the quiet."

Walter frowned. "What are you talking about?"

"You were dressed in leather and on a leash, and she was spanking you with a whip." Greg leaned on the wall and laughed heartily, "man, don't you know that you can't allow a girl to video tape you like that?"

Walter felt light-headed, he had forgotten all about the stupid videotape. He had been hopped up on ecstasy and Gia was fulfilling her fantasies as a dominatrix.

"Let me see it," he said to Greg forcefully.

"I don't have the phone, gave it back to Gia. I don't know how I am going to leverage her naked photos yet. But I will."

Walter sighed. "Greg, did you delete the video with me?"

"I was going to," Greg shrugged, "it wasn't very interesting not like the others where she is alone with her sex toys but here's the thing, I was checking the video out in class, and my teacher caught me.

"Next thing I know they took my phone away. Expect a call from the dean of discipline. The teacher who took the phone knows Gia's folks very well. When she saw the video, she looked like she was going to faint."

Walter inhaled raggedly. "Are you serious!"

"Yep," Greg said happily, "I heard the words expel, parents and Christian institution in the same breath. You are in trouble dude. For my part in this, I am sorry."

Greg didn't sound sorry.

Walter slumped on the wall. "When did this happen?"

"Yesterday." Greg gave him a jaunty salute and left.

Somehow Walter doubted that the teacher finding the video was an accident.

He had to talk to Gia and get her to delete the offending thing and then he had to call his brothers.

Preston was going to kill him. He couldn't even hope for Jordan's intervention in this one. It would be a terrible shame to be kicked out of school a year before graduation. He felt like a failure.

Chapter Seven

It rained all afternoon. It was almost six o'clock before Walter psyched himself up to see Gia. He wished the need to talk to her would never arise again, but here it was. He thought about what he would say but decided to just drive to her apartment, knock on her door and wing it.

He expected her to open the door in her regular skimpy get up and a sultry pose, instead someone yanked open his old apartment door.

It was a girl in braces and horn-rimmed glasses. She had dots of white cream all over her face, and she was in a thick bulky sweater and equally thick track pants. He couldn't discern a shape from the clothing, but she was medium height probably reached him at his shoulders.

Her hair was in some bright blue and green twirly things. He had no idea what they were called. He had seen other girls in them and when they took them out their hair was curly. She had a hair dryer in her hand, and she looked from him to Gia's door.

He cleared his throat and pushed his hand into his pocket. "Goodnight, does Gia still live here?"

"She does," the girl said, "but she is not in. You don't remember me, do you? First year, house party date? You disappeared on me."

"Gia's cousin, Aisha," Walter snapped his fingers. "Yes, that's right. I wasn't feeling the party vibe that night."

"Yep it's me, Aisha, you said my name was pretty." Aisha grinned. "I finally got a chance to live off campus on a trial basis unlike the Queen G, who has been living it up for a while."

"Do you have any idea when she'll be in?" Walter asked. "I need to talk to her."

"No idea," Aisha pushed her hand into her jacket. "Maybe I could tell her that you stopped by when I see her."

He didn't want Gia to think he was pursuing her. And he definitely didn't want to leave a message.

"No thanks. I think I'll just come back." Walter inhaled and then moved away from the door and almost collided with Gia.

"Walter Wiley, what a surprise!" Gia said in a fake high voice. "What brings you back to your old apartment building?"

"I came to see you," Walter said, he looked at her closer. She was looking a bit un Gia like. Her eyes were red she had obviously been crying, and her hair looked like it had gone through a wind tunnel. Despite her greeting, she looked vulnerable and depressed.

He had never seen her look so ruffled before.

He was curious as to why, but he wasn't going to get sucked into Gia's poisonous sphere anymore.

"Here I am," Gia said flippantly, "get a good eyeful."

"I want to talk to you," He said firmly.

Gia looked at him and then huffed, "I guess we have to."

Aisha looked between the two of them, curiosity in her gaze.

Gia opened her apartment door and looked at Aisha. "Hey, Aisha. You realize you still have acne cream all over your face? You weren't planning to go out like that?"

Aisha shrugged. "Maybe, what's it to you?"

Gia sighed. "Come on in, Walter. You were a much better neighbor than this one."

Walter hesitated. He didn't want to go into her apartment. He didn't want to be in an enclosed space with her, but he had to, they needed to have this conversation.

He glanced at Aisha who was still standing at her door and looking at him fixatedly before he entered behind Gia and closed the door.

Gia sat on her sofa and closed her eyes with a groan. "Trust me, Walter, I know why you are here. It's because of the video.

"I deleted the stupid thing from my stupid phone. I deleted all the videos and photos from my phone, but it won't do me any good. My dad just called me. He will be coming by in two days, the administration is involved. I am going to be in a ton load of trouble."

Walter inhaled tremulously, this means that he was going to be in trouble too. He had called Preston about the tape, and his brother had let him have it. He wished now that Jordan had been the one listed as his official guardian.

He pushed his hand into his pocket. "Well then, that's all I needed to hear. Bye."

"Wait, Walter!" Gia stood up quickly, "I miss you. I swear I didn't mean what I said about being bored or that I conquered you. I am so sorry."

Walter sighed. "Gia, you meant it. I will get boring if I stick around and God forbid, declare my love for you sometime in the future. Besides, you are too toxic for me. I have to think about my own emotional, spiritual and physical health. We are not compatible. You said you want bad. I am not bad. I tried it, didn't like it. Maybe you will be better off with an abusive thug with a very healthy disregard for you as a person.

"Or somebody who will slap you around roughly, I don't know, but I can tell you that I do not care. Keep your sorry."

He breathed out in relief when he left the apartment. He had always wanted to say that.

He felt a sense of relief so intense he leaned on the wall outside and took a deep breath in before he left the building.

****

He was not expelled from the school. Not because Preston had much clout with the administration but because Bishop Fire did.

They all watched the video on Greg's phone. It was tame enough compared to the others that Gia had taped with other people. Gia was the one who was really on trial for her multiple violations of school rules. She videotaped herself breaking most of the school rules.

When he heard her list of infractions, Walter was hopeful they would let him go. But the dean of discipline was treating him and the other students who were involved in Gia's videos as if they were accessories to a crime.

The dean wanted to expel him, and he was absolutely ready for it, but then the Bishop involved the President of the school and the head of the school board, and there was a closed door meeting and the next thing he knew, he was free to go.

Not before the dean said to him bitingly, "Stay far away from that girl Gia, she will ruin you."

He had nodded vigorously. He had already started living that advice months before.

Preston was not as easy on him. They had a discussion in the middle of the parking lot at the president's office.

Preston looked slightly tired around the eyes, and he had a slump to his shoulders.

"You cannot afford to be like this, Walter. You cannot afford these kinds of things to happen to you. You have to be more responsible."

He listened to the lecture and took it humbly. He had seen the sadness and concern in his brother's eyes and had vowed that he would never have the occasion to be the one who was lectured ever again.

He wasn't comfortable being the black sheep. He would fall in line.

****

Walter spent more time in the library than his dorm room during his final year at Mount Faith. He had a grade point average to boost and brothers to impress with his new and improved work ethic.

He was on his regular pilgrimage to the library when he collided with Aisha Fire at the door. They were both reaching for the door at the same time, and he knocked off her glasses and both their books went flying everywhere.

"Oh my," she muttered, squinting up in his general direction. "Sorry."

"My fault," Walter murmured. "I am very sorry."

He picked up her glasses and handed it to her and then

headed for the books.

He had completely forgotten about Aisha. She had not been a feature in Gia's life when he and Gia had their one-year relationship.

Aisha did not hang out with Gia, and he could understand why she was not good for Gia's ego.

He gathered the books in a pile, mixing up Aisha's and his. They seemed to be identical, Mathematics was a topic on all of them.

"You are doing Advanced Mathematics?" Walter asked when he went over to Aisha who had her glasses back on and was grinning at him.

"Walter!" Aisha hugged him with the books in his hands. And then stood back.

"How is it possible that you got better looking?"

Walter grinned. "Maybe you have better glasses?"

"Nope, I am wearing the same one, it's a good pair of glasses." Aisha blinked rapidly, the glasses gave her eyes a bug effect.

He found it cute. Walter tried not to smile.

"And yes, I am doing Advanced Mathematics." Aisha continued. "Tutoring it actually. I did it as a subject last year. Found it fun and decided to make some extra money instead of giving my services away for free."

"I could use some tutoring," Walter murmured, "I am drowning in the class."

"I charge by the hour," Aisha said briskly, "we could start now. My student for this hour canceled on me."

"Well then let's go." Walter definitely needed the help. "What is your major?"

"Mathematics, of course, the easiest subject on earth. What's yours?"

"Finance, emphasis on Accounting," Walter answered.

They reached the main floor of the library and then headed upstairs to the 'dead zone' which housed books from the science and mathematics departments.

It was usually fairly scanty and was often used for group work and discussions since nobody there normally found a little noise offensive.

There were only a few people there and he and Aisha headed to the very far end.

"Okay," Aisha said resting her knapsack on the table. "We have to work out a schedule."

Walter nodded.

"I know your syllabus. I can bring you up to speed in a matter of weeks."

Walter liked how efficient she sounded. "You sound confident, I like that in a tutor."

Aisha looked at him sternly over her glasses. She did her best schoolmarm interpretation. "I don't require you to like me, young man. We are here to learn, the clock starts now."

She slammed a stopwatch on the desk almost making him jump and then pulled out a test paper and handed it to him.

"You have thirty minutes. After you finish the paper, I will see in what areas you are weak."

Walter nodded vigorously, not daring to say anything else. Aisha got up and left him to it. He slowly went through the paper, knowing that he was going to flunk some of the questions, especially the ones related to statistics.

Aisha returned after thirty minutes graded his paper, declared him not nearly as brain dead as she had thought he would be and then proceeded to teach him.

She was an excellent teacher. And he told her that several times after she helped him to grasp a concept.

After the Advanced Mathematics class, which he passed with an A-, he found himself drifting into hanging out with

Aisha. She was so different from Gia.

She had a cluster of friends who were very spiritual and they had him involved in the youth ministry on campus. They visited other churches and did programs and even had a team-building exercise at an Easter church camp in Kingston.

That was how Aisha met Guy. He had attended the same camp; they had become fast friends because Aisha was her affable loving self.

There were no two ways about it, she was pretty close to being the best friend he ever had. Apart from his brothers, she had become very close to him especially during his last semester at Mount Faith.

She told him about her family. It was weird; he had been seeing Gia for a year, and he had never gotten more than a line or two about her family, the Fires. But Aisha told him everything.

The Fire siblings left Ethiopia in the seventies. Six brothers and three sisters. Several of the siblings went to Canada, Yonas Fire and his youngest sister Grace settled in Jamaica.

Yonas Fire became a bishop and founded his own church in Montego Bay.

Grace, Aisha's mother, shacked up with a man who did his business with the fringes of society.

While Aisha was telling him her story, she was devouring an ice cream messily, smooching her face in it. Some of it was on her nose, on her glasses handle, and on her eyebrows.

"My father was a dreamer." Aisha smirked, "you know one of those people that always had a good idea and then never does anything about it? That was him. They ended up living in the ghetto when one of his bright ideas bankrupted them."

"I know about being bankrupt." Walter shrugged. "But go on with your story."

"And then my father died. He got involved in a business venture with the wrong people and lost their money, we even lost our house in the ghetto. You know you are in bad shape when even the inner-city don't want you." Aisha sighed, "we were homeless for a while, living out of my mom's old Ford Escort and then she swallowed her pride, drove to Montego Bay from Kingston and begged her brother to have pity on us."

"And did he?" Walter asked.

"Oh yes," Aisha nodded vigorously, "he is Bishop Fire. He wouldn't turn away his own sister. We lived with him and Aunt Zoya for a while. I went to high school; my mom got married to a very nice man and lived in Kingston. She left me with the family because she did not want to uproot me from high school. Well, that and her stepson, Mark was nutty as a fruitcake, and he was living with them.

"He tried to kill me twice. I never vacation with my mom and stepdad unless Mark was heavily medicated."

Walter glanced at her sharply. "He tried to kill you?"

"Yep," Aisha nodded, "he has a mental disorder. He doesn't mean it. When he does not think that he is in another universe, he is a very sweet and lovable brother. In some ways better than Gia, who I suppose is sane.

"When my mom went back to Kingston, Gia, made my life hell. And she has no excuse."

"If I get a little attention from her parents. She throws a tantrum. I am two years younger, and I don't have a photographic memory, and yet still we ended up in the same classes in high school.

"Let me tell you, Gia hated that. At home, she tried everything in her power to diminish me in her mother's and father's eyes. At school, she tried to get me expelled. It was pathetic, her attempts. Luckily, most people saw through her stunts."

"Gia, Gia, Gia," Walter sighed, "she is something else."

"I concur." Aisha licked her fingers thoroughly and without inhibition. "Gia hates the fact that I got to come to college with her. I got a scholarship, and she didn't."

"So, tell me about you," Aisha said wiping her mouth on her napkin. "And don't leave anything out. How is it that you have no parents?"

"I had parents," Walter corrected her. "For years there was just my two brothers and me. I had no idea that we had other brothers or that my dad had another family. Maybe, vaguely, I knew that something was not right with my family. My mom was unhappy all the time, and my Dad was never home on weekends or holidays.

"And then Preston told me that we had a brother in his high school class that was the same age as him and that he looked like him. I wondered about it for a while. I asked my mom one day about it, and she went crazy. It was something to see. My once calm, collected mom turned into a really different person, someone from whom I had to keep secrets. And then my dad moved out to live with his other family, and we met them. I had more brothers than I had thought."

Walter took his napkin and wiped a blob of ice cream from Aisha's chin. "My mother couldn't handle my dad leaving. I think it may have made her unhinged. She killed my dad, his other lady and then herself."

Aisha gasped. "How old were you?"

"The grand old age of ten." Walter shuddered. "I never really grieved for any of it. I lost everything in a short space of time, my parents, the business, the house and I just shut it all out. I guess that is why I wasn't interested in girls."

Aisha looked at him in horror. "You don't like girls?"

"No." Walter shook his head. "I just never had an interest

in women. Not like other boys my age. I guess I was a case of arrested development."

He looked at Aisha guiltily, she had no idea about him and Gia. It was still amazing to him that the relationship with Gia had been mostly between them. They had spent most of their time in her apartment or the ridiculous parties she had dragged him to.

And then he realized with a jolt that he liked Aisha. Not just as a casual friend but as someone he could have a future with. There was something about her that unsettled something in him in a good way.

She was easy to talk to, she was witty and sweet and loved most of the things he loved. Her appearance belied her personality; she was not a nerd or unexciting in any way. She loved sports, she was a beast at the gym, she liked the same music that he did, well most of them anyway and she found his jokes funny.

He smiled at her, and she returned a shy smile as if she were reading his mind.

"Do you know the song Aicha by Cheb Khaled?" Walter tugged one of her braids.

"No." Aisha quirked a brow. "That's my name!"

"I can't believe that you don't know it. Are you serious?"

"Yes." Aisha nodded. "I never heard a song called Aicha. If I knew it, I would milk it for all it's worth. Does it say good things about us Aisha's."

Walter started singing it in French, no less. It took her a minute to figure out what language it was.

Aisha stared at him wide-eyed until he finished. "First of all, I have no idea what you just said, but you have a nice voice which is a complete shocker."

"The song says: As if I did not exist, she passed me by, without a glance, Queen of Saba. I said: Aisha, take, all is for you..."

"Queen of Saba?" Aisha whispered.

"Saba an old South Arabian Kingdom," Walter said easily.

"Okay, so this Aisha lived in a country without many women's rights. What does the rest of it mean?"

"After he offers Aisha all his treasures and is poetic to a fault." Walter grinned, "Aisha responds with, "Keep your treasures, Me, I'm worth more than that. Bars are still bars even if made of gold. I want the same rights as you and respect for each day, Me I want only love.""

"Wow!" Aisha whispered. "See I was right about the rights."

"Yep, but there is a response section to Aicha." Walter smiled, "the man says I want you Aisha and I love you to death, You are queen of my life and my love, You are my years and my life, I hope to live with you, only you."

"Oh my goodness, the words are so beautiful." Aisha was staring at him as if he was the bucket of ice cream in the cafe. She was almost salivating. "How do you know all this?"

"I memorized the song for French class. One of my favorite French language songs." Walter smiled. "I used to joke around that one day I would meet my Aisha. A woman who values love, equality, and freedom over worldly treasures. I really like the name, Aisha. It means life in Swahili, or woman in Arabic and that is why I told you that your name was pretty, kind of like you."

Aisha reached up before he could do anything else and kissed him on the lips.

Her lips were soft and pillow-like. He wanted to extend the kiss, but they were in a public place, and he had one strike against him already. Public kissing on the Christian university campus was frowned upon. He intended to graduate.

Aisha pulled away from him and then smiled. "You are

absolutely the best."

He smiled at her earnest declaration. He wondered if she would still think so after she heard about his relationship with Gia.

They hung out for the rest of the summer while Walter agonized whether to tell her about him and Gia. No moment was right to reveal the kind of sordid tale that had been his year with Gia.

He vowed to do it after graduation when he would officially ask Aisha to be his girlfriend.

But, he never got the chance to do so because Aisha graduated in absentia. She got the chance to tour Europe with an aunt of hers and almost simultaneously she got a Rhodes scholarship to study at Oxford University.

It had been a busy time for her and the wrong time to suggest a relationship. He would be fine with their friendship in the interim, but they never kept in touch. At least she never kept in touch. He had sent her emails, but she never responded.

****

She was back in his life almost at the same time as Gia and Axel.

Was all of this coincidence that she was back in his life just when he was in the middle of a slump and feeling restless about being alone, especially since his older brothers had coupled up and were having children?

He got up and reached for the phone. He was not going to sit and stew in his memories. He called Guy.

Guy answered on the first ring.

"I was just going to call you, but you beat me to it," Guy said, "would you like us to go over to Portland and see Uncle

Micky this weekend?"

"Yes," Walter said without pause. He would avoid church and get a reprieve from the inevitable confrontation with Gia and Axel.

"Really?" Guy asked skeptically, "I expected you to argue. None of you like to visit Uncle Micky."

"I need to escape this weekend." Walter sighed. "You won't believe this, but we are getting a new pastor."

"What happened to the old one?" Guy asked, "I liked him."

"Issues with church finances." Walter laughed dryly. "You didn't ask who the new one is going to be"

"Who is it?" Guy asked.

"Axel Parks and his lovely wife Gia Fire," Walter said it more bitterly than he intended.

Guy's gasp was loud in his ear. He didn't speak for a couple of seconds.

"Stop playing," he finally said.

"Not playing," Walter murmured. "When I heard I was shell-shocked it is just starting to sink in."

"My goodness," Guy muttered, "do the others know?"

"No, they are otherwise occupied." Walter groaned. "To be honest, I came home and wallowed in self-pity reminiscing about the past and then I called you. Wait, before that, I saw a light in your house and found out that you have a tenant."

"Aisha Fire," Guy chuckled. "I knew there was something I had to call you about. How does she look these days? Is she still wearing sneakers and long jeans skirts?"

"No. You won't believe how she looks if you see her now. She could give Gia a run for her money."

"That's my girl." Guy chuckled. "I knew she would come into her own one day."

"You kept in touch with her all this time and haven't seen her?" Walter asked incredulously.

"Yep," Guy said. "We occasionally text each other over the years. Aisha has a way of sticking with you."

"Yes," Walter murmured.

"She said that she was in dire straits and needed somewhere to crash. I left my spare keys at the store for her to pick up. She is a good person, completely unlike Gia."

"Do you think Gia has changed? I mean she married a pastor."

Guy cleared his throat. "For that matter, do you think he has changed? I mean how long have they been married? Are the little boys at church safe from him? How on earth did he end up with Gia Fire?"

Walter sighed. "I don't know. That's the million-dollar question. I won't let it keep me up tonight though."

He hung up the phone from Guy and changed into his gym clothes. He needed to work out in order to sleep.

Chapter Eight

The gym was state of the art and upgraded with the latest equipment, Walter had seen to that. He was the most avid user of the place. His sister-in-law, Sheryl visited consistently, but she was taking a break because of the pregnancy, most mornings she swam. Tonight he needed some hard cardio. He considered the pool for a while and then went on the treadmill. A hard run uphill would do him some good. He hoped he would be too exhausted to think.

He plugged in his earphone cranked up the music and ran like he could escape his past. He didn't realize that he had company until half an hour later.

Aisha was sitting on an exercise ball panting like she had just gone through a hard work out. He hadn't even realized that she was in the gym!

"Hey, I thought you were on a date." Walter grabbed a towel and wiped the sweat from his eyes.

"I went, came back, and couldn't sleep I saw the lights on

in here and decided to check it out." Aisha groaned. "I was trying to keep up with you on the treadmill. I did say hi when I came in, but you were caught up in your own world."

"Oh," Walter inhaled raggedly, "I guess I was."

"Have you called your brother about me yet?" Aisha asked batting her eyelashes at him and grinning.

"Yes," Walter nodded.

"Walter Wiley, I can't believe this, we live beside each other now! This is craziness!"

"Craziness," Walter observed her for longer than was comfortable. She started fidgeting. He didn't feel sorry for her discomfort. She deserved to squirm. She was the one who had gotten away, and he still had no idea why.

"You were er...you have a lot on your mind," Aisha said in the silence, "you were on autopilot on the treadmill. I tried to go as fast, and now I can't feel my legs."

Walter twisted his neck from side to side. "I don't feel tired. Maybe I should take a couple laps in the pool, that should wipe me out. I am going to shower."

"I should take a couple of laps too." Aisha got up, "I am going home to shower and change into my only pair of swimwear. I had no idea you people had a pool."

Walter nodded.

She was still the same Aisha though she had completely changed her look. It was slightly disconcerting; she looked different but felt the same.

Aisha had morphed into a sophisticated woman. Gone were the sneakers, long skirts and the hair in perpetual braids. She looked more like Gia but without the hauteur and coldness.

He wondered how else she had changed.

And he found himself floating in the pool and looking up at the night stars, contemplating it.

When he heard a splash near the left side of him. He looked

over at her. She grinned and gave him a thumbs up.

"The water is perfect. I was expecting it to be cold."

Walter swam over to her and pointed to where the thermometer was. "You can adjust the temperature from there."

"Okay." Aisha grinned at him, "I love this place. It's like a hotel. Guy has a housekeeper that comes in every day, and you have a pool and a gym. Goodness. When I leave here, I will be thoroughly unfit for regular apartment living."

"So why are you staying here?" Walter treaded water beside her.

"There was a fire at the place where I was supposed to live. Aisha sighed, "You heard about the fire at Dunrobin?"

Walter nodded. "Yes, new apartment building, they said a gas stove blew up."

"Yup. That was the place. The fire was in the apartment beside mine. I had just opened my trunk to take out my first box when I heard an explosion then the fire alarm sounded. Needless to say, most of the apartments on that floor are damaged."

"It's a good thing that you were not there at the time." Walter whistled. "The results would not have been pretty."

"Yes." Aisha nodded. "It was divine providence. There was a ton of traffic on the road that day, and I was impatient to get there. I will never again complain about traffic."

"So you had nowhere to live, and you called Guy?"

"Yes, I slept in my car, went to school the next day, and the VP allowed me to freshen up in one of the school cottages. And then I started thinking, I could stay with my mother and stepfather but they are on a cruise. They won't be back until next Wednesday. And there is no way I am staying at the house with only Mark there. I have no idea if he is on his meds and even if he were I would not chance it. Did I tell you he tried to kill me once? Thought I belonged to some secret organization that was watching him."

Walter nodded. "He is still delusional?"

"Sometimes," Aisha grimaced, "when he is not on his meds. My mom sneaks it into his morning juice."

"You could have called me," Walter said. "You know that I work at Wiley Corp."

"But you are an old friend, not exactly current." Aisha pulled herself out of the water and sat on the pool ledge. "I am suspicious of old friends contacting me out of the blue and asking favors. I guess you would be too."

He followed her on the ledge, putting a respectable distance between them and trying not to stare at her silky legs. Her bathing suit was modest enough, but she had a beguiling shape.

"Besides," Aisha continued, "what could be worse than calling someone out of the blue and begging them for help? It's tacky."

Walter opened his mouth to argue and then changed his mind.

"What do you teach?" He asked instead. He dragged his eyes from her legs and looked at her face instead.

"Guess." Aisha grinned at him.

"Mathematics." Walter chuckled. "Stupid question, huh?"

"Yup on both counts."

"All the hottest teachers are into numbers," Walter murmured. "All of them."

Aisha laughed. "Really now, I don't know about that, I had a hot English teacher. He was really good looking. All the girls wanted to take his class."

Walter chuckled. "Let me guess, you sat at the very front of class and drooled."

"No!" Aisha widened her eyes in horror, "Not me. I was

Bishop Fire's niece; I sat at the very back of the classroom and drooled."

Walter laughed out loud. "You are as humorous as ever."

"A woman without a sense of humor is like a brassiere without tits."

Walter howled with laughter.

Aisha chuckled. "That quote belongs to my mother by the way. If you want to steal it, please credit Grace Fire."

"I don't know when I would ever get the chance to use it." Walter wiped his eyes.

"I forgot how much I like talking to you, Walter. I should have ditched my date tonight and joined you at the gym sooner," Aisha said, "I forgot how much fun it was to hang with you."

"What happened to your date?" Walter asked. "You sounded excited about going."

"Greg does not get the concept of friends first. He thinks whispering lewd stuff in my ear is a turn on. And he keeps complimenting me and exclaiming, 'Oh my god, you are so pretty now. If I had known that you were going to turn out like this, I would have gotten first dibs in university.'"

"First dibs? He is still using that word?" Walter chuckled. "That's very mature of him."

"Dating in the twenty-first century is crazy," Aisha muttered, "crazy I tell you."

"Dating Greg is crazy, full stop. I warned you," Walter said. "But I guess you had to experience Greg for yourself."

"And I did." Aisha sighed. "You know what? I don't want to date anymore. I want to be courted. I am convinced that God said this is my year to get married, and I want the full works from my prospective husband. I want a good old-fashioned courting."

Walter nodded contemplatively. "And what does good old

fashioned courting entail?"

"You know, like flowers and nice outings, little gifts and chaste kisses, no assumptions of sex until marriage and poems and turning off the cellphones and other electronic gadgets when we are together. Can you believe that Greg checked his phone fifteen times tonight? I had to ask him if he was on call at his bakery."

Walter chuckled. "What did he say?"

"Just checking my messages, babe." Aisha imitated Greg accurately.

Walter grinned. "You have that spot on."

"That's another thing," Aisha said disgustingly. "I hate the nickname babe. I am nobody's babe. Say my name, it is a pretty name, Walter William Wiley says so!"

"And he is right." Walter smiled. "Have you listened to the song yet?"

"Nope, haven't heard it." Aisha shook her head. "Can you believe it?"

Walter changed the subject to a darker grimmer topic. "Did you know that Gia is in Kingston?"

"No." Aisha gasped, "the Queen G is here? What terrible news!"

"I take it you two don't keep in touch?" Walter frowned.

"Nope, she is squarely in the toxic family bin where I put most of my relatives who I only interact with out of sheer necessity. On top of that list is Gia. She is the only one on the list."

Aisha groaned, "I am going to have to move. I have a funny feeling Kingston is not big enough for both of us."

"What happened between you two?" Walter asked intrigued.

"She was awful to me growing up. We were never close you know that."

Walter nodded. "I know."

"Gia is...you know what, it doesn't matter anymore." Aisha shrugged a slim shoulder, "I stay far from Gia. My uncle talks to my mother occasionally, as usual, he has glowing reviews about his children. Gia included. Last I heard she was engaged to a pastor."

"She is married to my new church pastor." Walter sighed, "I can't believe that Gia is my first lady."

"Wow," Aisha widened her eyes, "you had a falling out with her too, didn't you?"

"Yes." Walter laughed dryly. "I haven't seen her yet though."

"Remind me not to visit." Aisha snorted, "I don't want to run into Gia."

"Maybe she has changed." Walter shrugged. "I am dearly hoping that she and her husband have gotten better with time. To be honest, I am kind of reluctant to go to church this weekend too. I am going to Portland with my brother Guy instead."

"Can I come with?" Aisha asked, "I have never been to that side of the island."

"Sure." Walter nodded. "We leave Friday evening at four."

"That's good, school ends at three." Aisha clapped her hands. I'll be here by three thirty the latest."

Walter slipped back into the water. "Race you to the end of the pool."

"Bring it on!" Aisha squealed. "You may rule the treadmill, but the pool is my domain!"

Chapter Nine

Aisha let herself inside the townhouse after saying goodnight to Walter and leaned on the door. It was ten minutes after one. She needed to be up by seven for school, but she did not care. As usual, Walter had been good company. He was perfect actually. If only he weren't gay.

She remembered the first time she had met Walter Wiley, it was the stupid date to some house party that Gia had felt obligated to take her along because she had not wanted Aisha to tell on her.

She had been stunned into immobility when she had seen Walter. Tall, caramel and handsome—really handsome. He was in a blue shirt, which showed off his well-defined biceps, and he had the kind of chiseled features that made him look like he won some kind of genetic lottery.

He had been worth the long stare and frozen stance. She had never seen anybody look like him in real life before and then she discovered that Walter was cool. Not full of himself or pompous in any way just cool.

The second time she saw him, he had come to the apartment to seek out Gia, her heart had sunk like a stone all the way down to her toes. How on earth did Gia do it? How did Gia get these men to act a fool for her? The only thing going for Gia was her looks. Beneath it all, she was as rotten as it was possible to be.

People usually found out in the long run. She had stood frozen in the doorway of her apartment wondering when Walter would eventually find out.

She couldn't look away from him as she babbled her way through reminding him that she was Gia's cousin and they had gone on a date together during their freshman year.

He had remembered her name because he thought it was pretty and she had hugged that knowledge over the year and a half as if it were some major privilege to be named Aisha.

He had gone into Gia's apartment when she had eventually shown up. And Aisha had stood outside, anxiously listening for him leaving.

He didn't even see her standing there when he exited the apartment. She had watched him walk away with her mouth slightly opened, but Gia had seen her at the door blinking after Walter in a daze.

"He is fine, isn't he?" Gia asked almost wistfully.

"Yes, he is," Aisha whispered. "Fine... Fine... Fine."

All the while she was thinking, please don't say he is your boyfriend but even if he were her boyfriend it would not have mattered, Gia changed boyfriends as often as she changed her underwear.

And then Gia had looked at her slyly. "Don't get your hopes up, he could never be interested in you."

"I know." Aisha had whispered stricken, which was ridiculous because she would never have a chance with a man like Walter, not in a million years. They usually ended up with the Gia's of this world—supermodel look-alikes with perfect bodies, perfect skin, and perfect teeth.

Her face was covered in acne cream, she had the most hideous braces to correct her double row teeth, and she was dressed in the most unattractive heavy clothes. She didn't have any cute winter clothes, and Mount Faith was constantly cold.

"That's right," Gia said giving her a warning stare. "Don't even think about him."

"I won't," Aisha said faintly, "I am not into torture I know when someone is unattainable."

"Good," Gia said happily. "Since you are my cousin and I don't want you to get hurt chasing somebody who will eventually hurt you, my advice is to stay away."

"Okay," Aisha frowned. It was kind of shocking to Aisha that Gia was even speaking to her in long coherent sentences. Usually, she got a token grunt or a growl.

"I wouldn't have a chance with him anyway," Aisha said trying to cheer up herself and projecting a casual attitude to Gia, "no chance at all."

"That's right," Gia said, "not a whisper of a chance. You didn't get much of the Fire genes, did you? All the women in our family are pretty but you...you got more of the Leonard's than you should. Your mother should have just called you Leonard so as not to sully the Fire family name. They say God doesn't make mistakes, but I think with you he could have been a little bit more generous in the looks department."

Aisha wrapped her arm around herself and wondered why she ever had a conversation with Gia, she always felt diminished and inadequate after her cousin was done with her.

But she wouldn't let her see it. She had long figured out

that Gia thrived on lashing out and she deliberately said hurtful things because she wanted to one day break her.

She gave Gia a wry smile. "God may have been short with me in the looks department, but he really did you a disservice in the personality department. Your personality is so ugly if your looks could switch places with it, people would run screaming when they see you."

Gia growled at her. "You are so rude."

"Right back at you Queen G," Aisha smirked. She went inside her apartment feeling ugly and disappointed.

She had seen Walter twice on campus after that. He was standing with a group of people at the library, and she had seen him laugh. As usual, she had stood aside and stared like an awestruck teenager, which she was. She had been nineteen. And she had a robust crush on Walter Wiley.

The collision at the library door was the happiest of coincidences; she must have been more shaken than she had originally thought because after straightening up and collecting her books from Walter, she acted like a confident unaffected female who was completely at ease around him.

But she hadn't been, not really. She was mostly in a daze of unbelief.

And when they became friends, each day she woke up pinching herself. She couldn't believe that Walter Wiley was her friend, closer to her than any girlfriend she had.

People even started referring to them as a couple. And she secretly fantasized that it was true.

But then came the opportunity of a lifetime. Her aunt Edna proposed a European trip tour, with her as a companion. She had felt both dread and excitement at the news. Dread because she would not see Walter for six whole weeks and excitement because it was Europe. Who would not want to go on a European tour?

Besides that she had eighteen months of Oxford to contend with, she was going to have a long distance relationship with Walter eventually, but they were so in sync that she had no doubt that they would be fine.

It was only at the mini family reunion and send-off party for her and Edna that she realized that she was living in cuckoo land.

Gia cornered her on the patio, her eyes blazing with hatred. "You are so pathetic!"

"Why?" Aisha asked smugly, "because I get to go to Europe and you are staying here?"

"No." Gia snarled, "because I told you to stay away from Walter and I see you two tight like peas in a pod walking around campus."

"Are you jealous?" Aisha laughed, "Walter does not seem to mind the ugly Fire cousin."

"No stupid," Gia had growled, "Walter is gay!"

Aisha still remembered the iciness in her palms. The sheer disbelief she felt.

"Gay, gay, gay," Gia said over and over and laughed in her face.

"Walter told me his secret. I am only telling you so that you don't do something stupid and fall for him. I did warn you before, but unfortunately, you think I am somehow jealous. "

"How do you even know if this is true?" Aisha stammered out the question.

"He lived beside me," Gia said slyly, "I have seen his visitors, heard the stuff they get up to, and he confessed it to me. You are in over your head, girly. All I have to say is cut it off with Walter cleanly, and whatever you do, don't let him know that I told you. I did promise I would not break his confidence, but you are family and an exception."

Aisha had whispered, "Thank you," though it had stuck in

her throat and gratitude was the last emotion she was feeling.

She had not believed a word of what Gia said, but then she remembered a conversation where Walter had said he had not been interested in girls.

To be honest, she had questions about him. Why was he still single? She hadn't seen him make an advance on a single girl while they spent time together or comment on anyone. He was quite comfortable with her, he liked to organize parties and had strong opinions about decoration, and she could talk to him about most girl related things, and he didn't bat an eye.

And the most powerful reason of all was that he was an ordinary friend to Gia. Every boy she knew eventually went haywire over Gia. Why was Walter the exception?

Because he was gay.

It was staring her in the face all along, and she hadn't seen it.

Needless to say, she had a less than happy time on her vacation. She wailed and whinged about Walter to Edna who had encouraged her to cut him off altogether. It had been tough. She had found herself writing Walter long letters about her trip but not posting them.

And now, tonight, eight years later she was reminded afresh how much fun it was to be around Walter. He was easy to talk to and so relatable. It was freshly heartbreaking to find out he was not interested in women.

It was a waste. A serious and colossal waste. Aisha thought in despair. She went into her luxurious guest room and sat down on the bed.

Life could be so unfair. Whenever she liked a guy or felt a connection, something would always be wrong them. In her earlier years, if she liked a guy or anyone had even the remotest interest in her, Gia would deliberately seduce them away.

In her later years, it was one thing after another. They were either married already, wanted to have sex on the first date or if they were especially perfect like Walter, gay.

She breathed out raggedly. Walter... Walter... Walter. Like a mantra, she whispered his name.

When she had prayed about finding a husband and God had said this year she had no idea she would be thrust back into the space of the man that she had loved eight years ago.

And now here she was with Walter back in her radius. Her fascination with him had not dimmed, not even a notch, she refused to call what she felt love, but it was still as alive as ever

Her only saving grace through the years was that she was not in the same vicinity as him, but all that had changed now.

How was she going to find her husband when he was in the limelight of her emotions? How could she concentrate on anyone else and how was she supposed to act around him?

She looked at her watch before turning off her light. She knew without a doubt that she was going to dream about Walter.

She was still as pathetic as ever.

Chapter Ten

Walter woke up early on Wednesday morning despite how late he had gone to bed. He decided to get dressed for the office and get a head start on his day. When he looked at his clock in the hallway on his way to the kitchen, it was just about six-thirty. He didn't eat that early. He would just grab a cup of dandelion root tea, Sheryl had introduced it to him, and he found that it worked better than coffee to wake him up.

He was not too surprised when he heard his doorbell just as he was about to take his first sip. Jordan and Preston were on his step.

"Guy called you," he said when he opened the front door.

"Yes." Jordan frowned, "why didn't you tell us?"

"Because you were all busy with your families and I went to the gym to work it out, and I was chatting with our new neighbor, Aisha Fire until late into the night."

"How is Aisha settling in?" Preston smiled. "I glimpsed

her moving in yesterday."

"She is doing fine. Come on in," Walter left the door opened.

Preston and Jordan followed.

Walter offered them tea. They both declined. Jordan was the more impatient of the two. They wanted him to start talking.

"Come on, spill it. Tell us how your two worst nightmares are in town."

Walter told them of his first time hearing about Gia and Axel and how he reacted.

"I feel kind of stupid now," he shrugged, "but I was shocked out of my wits."

"That sicko is still practicing theology and calling himself a minister?" Jordan whispered. "We should give him the beating we didn't a couple years ago."

Preston shook his head, "Nope, you stopped me ten years ago, I'll stop you now. The better thing to do is to announce to the church what kind of past he has and let them decide if they want their little boys near the pervert."

"Maybe he is no longer a pervert, he is married to Gia, and she is not shy where sex is concerned." Walter shrugged. "Do you believe that once a pervert always a pervert? We had a discussion about redemption in elder's meeting, and I am giving the man the benefit of the doubt. And please remember, I am the one who he almost drugged and raped, and that is not something I want to be broadcasted to the world."

Preston grunted. "Well, people change. "

"Speaking of change. I wonder how Gia is these days. What kind of first lady will she be?" Jordan mused.

Preston snorted. "I will never forget the state that Gia put Walter in. We almost lost him. Axel was bad, but Gia Fire pushed him down to another level."

Jordan sighed. "Oh, she did."

"I am so happy that Pete forced Sheryl and I to go to the East Road church a couple months ago when he became the junior choir director. It was easier to switch churches than to drop him off at East Road and then pick him up again. If not, I would seriously be looking into switching right about now."

Jordan nodded. "I can easily switch, I have no church affiliations, and neither does Shawn. But that Gia she was a player, a mean player," Jordan murmured. "What are the odds, the two people who almost derailed your life, are now back in it and somehow got married to each other and are going to be the spiritual leaders in your church?"

"There has a sense of unrealness about it." Jordan shook his head. "I was up all night last night with Courtney. Maybe, I am sleep deprived and dreaming all of this because it can't be true."

"It is true." Walter stood up and washed out his cup. "What happened to Courtney?"

"She is the most restless baby on the planet." Jordan shook his head, "that child is going to drive me crazy. She is her mother's child through and through."

Preston and Walter laughed.

"Don't let Shawn hear you say that," Walter warned.

"Oh I told her several times last night," Jordan chuckled, "that I wouldn't exchange either of them for the world, as drama-filled as they both are."

"I know," Walter said wistfully. "I need a Shawn or a Sheryl in my life."

Preston nodded. "Or maybe an Aisha?"

"Aisha stonewalled me years ago. She left for Europe and basically stopped answering my mail." Walter snorted. "She has no interest in me whatsoever. I guess I am not her type."

"Or she knew that you and her cousin had a thing and is being cautious." Preston shrugged. "Eight years ago is a long time. Who knows what can happen now?"

"I still can't wrap my mind around this Axel thing though." Jordan whistled. "It literally boggles the mind. Has he really changed? Is he straight now? Was he gay, bisexual or what?"

Preston frowned. "I tell you, I am more shocked about First Lady Gia? Church life should be very interesting from now on for you Walter. That is if you are going to stay there."

"I have to." Walter rubbed the back of his neck absently. "I am very involved in quite a few things there. I have a reprieve this weekend though. I am going to Uncle Micky's in Portland with Guy. You should come. Guy thinks we don't spend enough time with Micky."

"I agree." Jordan nodded, "but this weekend, I have a funeral to attend all the way in Trelawny. One of my laborers' grandfather died. Have to show some support."

"If only Micky would come to town, we would see him more often," Preston said, "but this weekend they might induce Sheryl which means I will be a father again by Sunday."

Walter smiled. "I can't believe it, my big brother is going to be a father of two."

"Believe it, not only that," Preston sighed, "Pete is so girl crazy now, I may soon be a grandfather."

Walter laughed out loud. "Preston, the grandfather."

Jordan got up and yawned. "Tell me about Aisha. How close is she to Gia?"

"She is not close to Gia at all," Walter said. "They have a complicated relationship."

"But she is still Gia's cousin. Be cautious." Jordan warned as he headed to the door.

"I didn't say I liked her." Walter protested. "No need for a warning."

Preston looked through the window. "I never got a good look at her yesterday. Is that her in your walkway?"

Walter went over to the window and saw Aisha in a pinstripe suit with a briefcase in hand looking over at his house. She looked like she was undecided about something. Like she wasn't sure if she should knock on his door.

She was juggling her keys in one hand and biting her lip. Her hair was slicked back in a bun, and she had two curly tendrils at the side of her ears. She looked prettier than she had looked in the half dark last night and much better than he could have imagined from their friendship years ago. Then she had the proclivity for baggy clothes that swamped her figure and thick horn-rimmed glasses that covered half of her face.

In the early morning sunlight, he could see subtle brown streaks in her hair. Without the glasses, he could see the tiniest slant at the corner of her medium brown eyes and perfectly straight and aligned teeth when she greeted Jordan shyly.

"She is pretty, and you like her," Preston said beside him. "Let's hope she is nothing like her cousin, the evil Gia, your new first lady. I don't know if I'll get used to saying that. First lady, Gia."

Walter watched while Jordan met her. They spoke for a minute and then Jordan nodded to the townhouse.

Aisha made her way to his front door.

"I am going," Preston sighed, "update me with the crazy stuff going on in your life, okay?"

"Yes, sure." Walter followed him to the door and then leaned on it casually.

"Good morning Aisha."

"Hey," Aisha smiled, "I...hey," she looked at Preston and back to Walter. "I er good morning. You have more company?"

"The name is Preston Wiley," Preston smiled at Aisha. "Welcome to our neighborhood. Guy called last night and told me you were here. We are a good bunch of neighbors. Call on any of us if you need anything."

"Thank you," Aisha nodded.

They watched as Preston walked down the walkway and across to his house.

"I know this is an imposition," Aisha whispered looking at Walter and trying not to stare at him too long. The man was simply spectacular in a suit. Like he was with no shirt on and in swimming trunks. She had dreamed about him last night, as she knew she would.

"I er...my car won't start," She said in a rush.

Walter smiled at her. "You don't have to whisper. How may I help?"

"I am running late, I didn't even know if you were up." Aisha sighed, "I would call a taxi but..."

"Say no more," Walter said, "come on in, I have to get my stuff and then I'll drop you at work. I'll arrange to have your car sorted out today."

"Thank you." Aisha gushed, "I am so sorry about this."

"Don't be," Walter said as he headed into his living room. "You heard my brother, we are good neighbors."

Aisha sat down on the edge of a sofa and looked around. The layout for Walter's house was slightly different from the layout at Guy's place his living room was to the left; Walter's to the right, and the decor was noticeably different.

Guy's place had a lighter more modern feel, with light mint green walls and white crown moldings and baseboards. Walter's place was painted in darker earth tone colors with cut stone accent walls, and his living room opened up to a patio that looked out onto a gorgeous oasis.

"I am going upstairs for my work stuff," Walter said to her. "Be back in a jiffy."

"Sure," Aisha said heading for the glass doors, "your patio is gorg. I mean really gorg, look at those plants and the waterfall."

"My sister-in-law, Shawn designed it," Walter grinned. "I told her to recreate the Garden of Eden in my 600 square feet of space, and that is what she did. I like to throw dinner parties, it is a conversation piece.

"It sure is," Aisha turned back to the patio, "I guess you spend most of your time out here."

"More or less," Walter said. "I'll invite you to dinner one night."

"That would be great." Aisha smiled at him.

His phone rang while he was on his way back downstairs. He answered it.

"Elder Walter, it's Mary here. My food warmers are malfunctioning, and the welcoming party for the pastor is tomorrow night. Can I borrow yours?"

Walter sighed.

He wanted to say no. He didn't want anything of his, even inanimate objects to be a part of a welcoming party for Axel and Gia.

"Please Elder Walter, I am quite desperate at the moment."

"Okay," Walter said grudgingly. "I'll be passing your place this morning, I will drop them off then."

"Thank you, God bless you." Mary gushed. "Are you coming to the party?"

"No," Walter said solemnly. "Just no."

"One day you must tell me what this is about, Walter," Mary said grimly. "I deserve to know why the friendliest, outgoing elder I know is so dead set against this new pastoral couple."

****

It couldn't be avoided. Walter stopped at Elder Mary's place with Aisha in the car. It was meant to be a quick stop, but Mary came out to greet them, her grandson Ivan was behind her with an accounting ledger.

"Ivan wanted to ask you to look over an accounting problem he has," Mary said, "It won't take five minutes. This is a critical grade. He is flunking accounts."

She looked in the car and saw Aisha and clapped her hands. "Oh, you have company?"

"My neighbor," Walter said, Aisha Fire. "She is a teacher, and I am dropping her to work this morning."

"Goodness," Mary whistled, "Fire. I had no idea it was such a popular surname."

Walter sighed. "It's not, as far as I know."

Mary drifted closer to the car. "You mean this lovely lady is related to our new first lady?"

Walter didn't answer, he left Mary to her investigation. He felt a jolt of sympathy for Aisha. When Mary was in information gathering mode, she was ruthless.

Ivan helped him to take the food warmers into Mary's cavernous kitchen. There was a dining area with a long table that could seat twenty.

Mary had a whole slew of children and grandchildren; he had no doubt that on a holiday that was not enough space for her brood.

"Okay," Walter turned to Ivan, "let me see that accounting ledger."

Ivan handed him the ledger and sat down at the island.

"I hate accounts and mathematics and anything that has anything to do with numbers."

Walter smiled. "That's a common attitude."

Ivan grinned. "I don't know how you do it, Elder Walter, you stare at numbers all day."

"Actually no," Walter said, "I oversee the people who stare at numbers all day. My day is usually filled with meetings and strategic planning sessions. Like today, in approximately one hour I have a planning session with other department heads and then a meeting with my accounting staff."

"That's cool," Ivan whispered. "I want a staff."

Walter laughed and pointed at the ledger. "Work on it. By the way, you have several mistakes in this problem. Here, here and here."

"Cool," Ivan grabbed his pencil, "you didn't even look at it long. I have been looking for the problem all night."

"I always had a knack for this kind of thing," Walter said, "I can spot an accounting problem with my eyes half closed. Don't worry, with practice you should be able to pick up on these things quite easily."

"Yeah," Ivan groaned, "Practice. I don't know where to start."

"I'll be teaching Accounts on Thursday's at the homework program at church. Make sure you are there."

"Oh, yes." Ivan nodded vigorously, "I have to be there or grandma will kill me."

When Walter reached the car, Mary was in earnest conversation with Aisha.

"Has Walter told you his secret?" Mary asked when Walter got in the car.

"No," Aisha glanced at him and then cleared her throat. "He hasn't told me anything."

"He is quite tight-lipped about it," Mary said mockingly,

"doesn't want anyone to know. Don't forget to visit our church while you are here in Kingston. It is the warmest, friendliest place to worship. I will be mad if I don't see you with Elder Walter."

"I won't be there this weekend." Walter glanced at his watch, "I am going to Portland."

"Say hello to Pastor Tate for me, if you see him," Mary said warmly.

"I will, but I am not planning to go to his side of the parish." Walter started the car. "Have a good day, Mary."

"You have a good day too and thanks again for the warmers."

Walter drove off. He felt Aisha looking at him furtively.

He caught her when they stopped at the traffic lights. "What is it?"

"Nothing, I..." Aisha bit her lip. She was going to ask him if everybody knew he was gay. Instead, she said. "Your church is quite liberal, aren't they?

"Liberal? No." Walter chuckled, "how on earth did you get that idea? Definitely not from Mary. She is a tried and true, dyed in the wool conservative. She would beat you with the Bible if she could."

"And she knows your secret?" Aisha asked incredulously. "I would say she is tolerant and pretty liberal to know and not have a heart attack about it."

Walter sighed. "Mary doesn't know anything. She is just fishing. What did you tell her?"

"Nothing," Aisha said. "I didn't know that you knew that I knew."

"Huh?" Walter raised an eyebrow. "I figured Gia told you sometime through the years."

"Yes, she did tell me," Aisha said her heart sinking.

So it was true.

Somehow she was hoping it was not true. There was chemistry between her and Walter. There had always been chemistry between them. She could feel it even now. In her stupid mind, it was palpable and back in full force.

How could she have chemistry with a man who loved other men? She could swear that he felt attracted to her too. How could she be so way off?

"Do your brothers know?" Aisha whispered the question. She was still reeling from a sense of loss so intense she felt like crying. She really liked Walter Wiley. Why did he have to be gay?

"Yes." Walter frowned. "But I don't want anyone else to know, especially now. I am an elder at the church, the situation would be very awkward now, don't you think?"

"Yes." Aisha inhaled raggedly. "But how can you be a leader in the church with this er..." she cleared her throat. "How did they allow you to be an elder?"

Walter glanced at her quickly and then at the road. "I was appointed two years before this. Obviously, I had no idea that Gia and her husband would be at my church one day. If I knew, I wouldn't take up the position; I was nominated for it last year. I am now going to have to attend church board meetings with Axel Parks."

"I can't think of anything worse." Walter drove up to the school gates. "It will be an eventful couple of weeks ahead."

Aisha got out of the car and looked at Walter sadly. "Thank you for the lift."

Walter was a bit puzzled, why did she look like somebody had kicked her cat?

"It's no problem. I'll have someone sort out your car for you."

"Don't bother, I'll have my stepdad take care of it."

"Oh yes," Walter nodded, "I keep forgetting you are related

to the Anton Bull King from Bull Auto parts and Services."

Aisha watched him drive away. He was helpful, kind, easy to talk to, handsome and unavailable.

She walked into the schoolyard with a heavy heart.

Chapter Eleven

Aisha wished she had not invited herself along to Walter's Portland trip. She drove into the townhouse complex and parked in front of Guy's place. It was Friday, and she was feeling slightly off.

She just wanted to go to her bed and lie down and not get up until Monday morning. What was the use of being in Walter's sphere again? It made no sense.

She didn't want to fall for him all over again. She had moved on with her life. What she should be doing is keep her distance and thereby quickly get over her crush or whatever this feeling for him was.

She should not be ingratiating herself into his life and get close to him and fall into a hole of her own making.

She was not her mother.

Her poor mother had been a sucker for men who were closed off to her emotionally, men who she thought she could change. Aisha was not going down that route. In all her years of watching her mother's car crash relationships, she had made a vow never to get trapped in that sort of thinking.

She was very sure that people can change, but if they did, they had to do it themselves. They had to want to do it. They had to work on it. They had to be the force behind their own transformation.

Her mother had eventually lucked out and found a man who didn't have any issues but only after kissing one frog after another after another.

"Hey!" Walter knocked on her window.

She snapped out of her reverie and wound down the window.

"You okay?" Walter asked. "You parked the car and then sat there for a couple of minutes just staring transfixed through the window."

"I, ah," Aisha cleared her throat, "I was just thinking."

"Are you still coming to Portland with us?" Walter raised an eyebrow. "We leave in an hour."

Aisha swallowed. "I was thinking about that, maybe I shouldn't go."

"Why?" Walter frowned, "I was looking forward to you coming with us. Guy and I will be perfect gentlemen I promise."

"I know you will." Aisha closed her eyes and then opened them again. "I was just feeling a bit tired that's all."

"Don't worry the Upper Rio Grande valleys has a way to rejuvenate you, connect you with nature and remind you of the things that truly matter. At my uncle Micky's place there is no television, no cell phone towers, the man does not have electricity."

Walter grinned. "The place is a bit rustic but trust me, it has some of the most beautiful sunrises and Myrtle promised to cook. Myrtle Wiley is the best cook in deep rural Jamaica.

he still cooks on wood fire and bakes in an old style clay oven. You have to see it to believe it."

Aisha shook herself out of her doldrums, what was she getting so worked up about, this was Walter, he was gay, her crush couldn't last forever, could it? Eventually, she would see him as a friend.

"Okay. "Aisha smiled. "I am sold. I have to go and pack."

"Bring hiking gear," Walter said, "the Rio Grande Valley is nestled between Blue Mountain and John Crow Mountain, trust me when I say you are in for a treat."

Walter walked away, he was dressed in jeans and a white t-shirt that showed off his impressive biceps.

Aisha swallowed. There was no way on earth she was going to be just good friends with this man.

No way. She would spend all her time drooling, and it would be super unhealthy for her peace of mind.

Walter turned back and caught her staring at him like a lovesick puppy. "Bring a sweater, it gets really chilly in the mornings."

"Sounds like fun," Aisha said awkwardly. What on earth had she signed up for?

****

The journey to Portland was quite lively. Aisha was happy she hadn't change her mind. Guy had grown into his looks she stared at him in confusion. Eight years ago he had not looked this good.

The other brothers, Preston, Jordan, and Walter pretty much looked alike. They were handsome guys without a doubt, but Guy was verging on beautiful. She had no other way to describe him. He had long curly hair and finely chiseled features as if God had sat down and decided to pay him some extra attention—broad forehead, aquiline nose, hooded eyes which were a dark brown under thick black brows, smooth nutmeg shade skin and dark red lips.

She stared at him for so long that he cleared his throat. It wasn't that she was attracted to him or anything, but Guy Wiley deserved a thorough look.

"Earth to Aisha." His voice was slightly husky and smooth.

"Yes, I am here," Aisha shook her head, "you look different, taller, thicker, prettier."

Guy laughed. "Prettier? Oh, Aisha, you are going to give me a complex."

"Sorry," Aisha grinned. "You look different."

"Thanks." Guy grinned, "I have to say the same for you. You were always pretty, but I guess now you are allowing it to show. You got a makeover?"

It was Aisha's turn to blush. "Well sort of, after graduation I got fitted for contacts, my braces changed to retainers, and I took a design course a couple years ago and became clothes and shoes mad. The feminine kicked in."

Guy chuckled. "And in the process, you start giving Gia a run for her money."

Aisha shook her head. "I am not in Gia's league."

"No," Guy smiled, "you are better. You were always more beautiful inside and out. I am happy you are back in Kingston. You can stay at my apartment for as long as you like."

"Thank you," Aisha smiled. She wondered for a brief moment if he was the one for her.

And then Walter came out of his apartment with a backpack slung over one shoulder and the low humming attraction that was never far, hit her afresh.

It was amazing how this attraction thing worked. And how wrong her signals were. Walter the gay one had her attention without even trying. All he had to do was breathe, and her temperature rose.

Guy, gorgeous straight Guy did nothing for her.

She didn't like herself much at that moment.

Walter looked at the vehicle that Guy had parked in his driveway.

It was quite literally a rust bucket. It was obviously old and battered and in need of a paint job.

"I am not going anywhere in that," Walter said shaking his head. "What happened to your new Mercedes SUV?"

Guy grinned. "I am trying to impress a girl."

"In that?" Walter pointed to the vehicle baffled. "Which girl is this? A blind girl? She needs to hear you coming from afar?"

Guy laughed again and slapped the vehicle. "No. But showing up in anything classy will make her like me, and I want her to like me as a poor farmer. It's an experiment."

Walter sighed and looked at Aisha. "Do you want us to travel in my car?"

"No," Aisha smiled, "the rust bucket is fine. I want to hear more about this experiment."

Walter groaned. "Very well, let's go."

They were well on their way past Kingston and chugging up the steep inclines in Stony Hill before they started talking about Guy's experiment.

"So there is this lady in the valleys," Guy said, "she has two boys and one girl, her husband died about five years ago, and she moved to the Uncle Micky's section of the valley into a very run down house at the edge of the village.

"They are dirt poor. I mean dirt poor, no flooring in the old house. Guy sighed. Anyway, Uncle Micky and the rest of the community helped her out with food and clothing for the children, mostly hand me downs. They are never hungry or lack clothing, but their education was touch and go for a while. Until I stepped in, anonymously of course. I built a cottage for them, called myself the Farm Help Society."

Walter laughed. "Really?"

"I couldn't come up with a better charity sounding name," Guy said sheepishly. "Anyway, the Farm Help Society sent all three children to school. The oldest boy Earl is now twenty-one. I sent him to training school when he finished high school. He is doing electrical work and is quite good at it. He is earning money for himself and is building his clientele and contributing to the household.

"The other son, Nate is still in high school, this is his last year, he is bright, straight A's. The Farm Help Society will be sponsoring him through university. He wants to be a doctor."

"And the girl?" Walter asked. "What's going on with her?"

"Lucia is twenty," Guy murmured, "and quite a beauty. She finished high school and two years of community college. The Farm Help Society may have gotten her a job at the Wiley Groceries in Port Antonio as a cashier and gave her a camera as a birthday gift. She is artistically inclined, loves to take photographs."

Aisha chuckled.

"And the Farm Help Society may have warned off all the men in the district to leave her alone." Guy grinned. "The Society doesn't want her to follow the girls in the district and become a mother too soon with a million kids and a thousand baby fathers. It would be a waste of her life."

"Because the Farm Help Society wants her for himself." Walter laughed, "I think the Farm Help Society should leave the girl alone and stop directing her life like a choirmaster."

"Too late, I like her," Guy murmured. "And I think she likes me too, but I am a poor farmer and not upwardly mobile. I haven't exactly given her any reason to assume otherwise. I drive this rust bucket when I am visiting, and I am usually in the fields with the farmers. She hates the farming life. She is itching to leave the valleys. She thinks it is a death sentence."

Walter whistled. "Oh what a tangled web we weave."

Guy grunted. "Then there is this doctor that recently moved into the community who is making the moves on her. I now have serious competition, and I haven't finished my social experiment. Not to mention her mother is encouraging her towards the doctor, though I think Lucia likes me."

Aisha smiled. "I would love to hear how this ends."

"Sure," Guy said, "it could take a while though. Her mother is a formidable opponent, and she is working against me."

"I think you should stop the experiment and tell this girl and her mother that you are really the Farm Help Society and one of her bosses at Wiley Groceries and be done with it," Walter said. "Life is too short for games."

"Nah," Guy shook his head, "I want her to want me for myself, a poor farmer and then I can trust her enough to tell her the rest. Otherwise, I'll never be sure."

"Madness," Walter grumbled. "She'll marry the doctor and be gone before you know it."

Guy glanced around at Aisha. "Who would you choose, Aisha? Me or the doctor, if you were Lucia?"

Aisha chuckled. "You are very handsome. I am not sure. I'd have to see the doctor, measure how I feel, the chemistry and all of that. I'd choose who I have the greater spark with you know, but that's me. I was never dirt poor. I don't know if that what would motivate my choice in this scenario."

It was Walter's turn to look at her. "Chemistry over looks and money interesting."

Aisha made a face. "But I don't know if chemistry would be enough. My mother's relationships in the early years were mostly about chemistry, and they never ended well. I think she married Bull based on both chemistry and the fact that he could provide for her. They are happy together. So I guess a balance is necessary."

"How did your mother end up marrying Anton 'Bulldozer' King?" Guy whistled. "He is a giant of a man. He must be at least seven feet tall."

Aisha chuckled. "My mom took her old vehicle to be serviced at his Auto place in Montego Bay. She says, he took one look at her and asked, 'are you single?'

"She said yes. And he said, 'I am single too. My wife died two years ago, I have four children, one of them is crazy as a bat, and he lives with me. That could be an issue, so I am just putting it out there.'

"And my mom said, 'what are you talking about?'

"And Bull said, 'I clean up well, don't worry about the grease stains on my hand. I am going to marry you. I can feel it.'

"Four weeks later they were married. Fourteen years later they still act like newlyweds."

Walter laughed. "You told me this before, I remember thinking that Bull just got to the point."

"That's his personality." Aisha nodded, "he is direct like that."

"Maybe you should try that with Lucia," Walter mused, "and stop the experimenting."

Guy laughed. "We'll see."

Aisha looked between Guy and Walter. "You know. You two look so different, except for the hooded eyes."

"Joseph Wiley's eyes," Walter said, "we all got it from him."

"He was seriously handsome wasn't he?" Aisha whispered.

"Yes," Walter grinned, "I'll show you a picture when we

reach Uncle Micky's. Preston and Jordan are dead ringers of him."

"Preston and Jordan could be twins. Are you sure they have different mothers?"

"Yup, we are sure." Guy glanced at her, "Jordan cuts his hair low, that's why you can't see the curls like mine. I decided to grow my hair on a whim couple years ago."

"It's gorgeous," Aisha whispered.

"Stop lusting after my brother," Walter turned and grinned at her, "you like me, remember?"

Aisha laughed. "I am not lusting, just stating a fact and maybe I am a slight bit envious. He has gorgeous hair."

Guy laughed. "Thank you for the compliment, Aisha. You know you are nothing like your cousin, Gia."

Walter grunted. "We are trying to forget Gia this weekend, remember?"

****

Uncle Micky's house was at a place called Bowden Pen. It was a large wood cabin with a wrap around front veranda. It was situated on top of a hill.

The Blue Mountains loomed large above the hill with white clouds hugging the tips. At the bottom of Micky's hill was the Rio Grande. From that vantage point, it could be seen snaking its way through the lush green that lined its banks on both sides for miles.

Aisha had not stopped exclaiming since she arrived in the area. There wasn't one word to describe that side of Jamaica, but a few came to mind, lush, unspoiled, old world. She felt as if she had stepped back a couple of decades into time. It was obviously a farming community. The houses were mainly made of board, the people were friendly, they stopped and waved to Guy as he made his way through the village littered with banana trees. They had even passed a boy on a donkey as he made his way on the rain-slicked road.

"He is probably heading home from the market," Guy muttered. "Today is market day."

"It's so nice up here," Aisha murmured. She had wound down the windows completely even though there was a slight drizzle.

The air smelled pure and crisp. There was hardly any vehicular traffic once they turned off onto Bowden Road and still none when they made their way up to Mickey Wiley's cabin style house.

She had expected Mickey to be a withered old man, but she was mistaken. Walter and Guy had told her some things about him while they were on the way. He was a perpetual bachelor who was resistant to any modern changes to his environment. He had numerous conspiracy theories that he held dear. His favorite past time was drinking white rum after a day on the farm.

His cousin, Myrtle Wiley, lived with him and she did all of the cooking and cleaning. Myrtle greeted them jubilantly; she was a tall and muscular woman with what Aisha thought of as a strong angular face.

As if her face had weathered many a storm and had come out battered and dented up. When she smiled though it changed things, she looked attractive.

Mickey was the opposite. He was surprisingly good looking. He had a straight as an arrow nose with a bump in the middle, as if it had been broken at one time. He had a mostly unlined face and grey dreadlocks down that he had clipped up in a thong that reached him to his waist and he wore a colorful tam on the top of it. He was wiry and short and smelled like marijuana. He was more reserved in his greeting, but he grinned wide when he shook her hand.

"Welcome Miss Aisha."

Myrtle showed her to her room. It was simply decorated like the rest of the place. There were no frills, just a basic double bed, and a nightstand with a Home Sweet Home lamp that was filled with kerosene oil. There was a chest of drawers and a tiny closet area that had some racks.

The entire place had the same shade of medium brown wood. The only splash of color was the red, yellow and green comforter on the bed.

"You are going to need it," Myrtle said. "It gets very chilly in the nights."

There was even an ensuite bathroom. Myrtle showed it to her with pride. "We have running water now, Guy insisted on it couple years ago after he installed the tank. We even have a solar heater, so hot water is here too. The hot water is one of those things you never knew you missed until you have it."

Aisha nodded. "It's nice."

"I hope you are hungry, we have dinner in twenty minutes," Myrtle said heading outside, "I know Guy didn't stop for snacks, he knows not to eat before he gets here."

Aisha nodded. "I am famished." Myrtle was right, they had not stopped though it was a three-hour drive.

She sat on the bed and looked through the window at the winding waters of the Rio Grande and inhaled. There was a glorious sunset. She was happy that she decided to come along with Walter.

It was ridiculous how close she felt to him. It was as if eight years apart did nothing to dull her interest in Walter.

Chapter Twelve

"**S**unrise," Walter whispered in the early morning air. He had woken Aisha up at the crack of dawn, and they were seated on the back veranda looking towards the horizon.

"You haven't lived until you have seen a Rio Grande Valley sunrise." Walter murmured. "It is spectacular."

Aisha shuddered beside him in her sweater it was a little bit too chilly for her liking. "I slept like a baby last night. I had no idea I would. I went to bed at eight o'clock. Unheard of."

Walter chuckled. "It is the way our foreparents used to do it. Early to bed early to rise. No electricity. No city life. No television or cell phones."

"And there it is," Walter whispered, when the sun danced with the dark clouds on the horizon, creating bands of light and dark patterns on the pale blue sky. "Morning has broken."

Aisha glanced at him and then back at the beautiful vista. "It is glorious. I have never watched the sunrise with a guy before."

Walter looked at her and smiled. "And I can't think of anybody I would rather watch the sunrise with. You are good company, Aisha Fire. I think we could rekindle our friendship."

Aisha looked at him for a long silent loaded moment before nodding. "Yes, maybe."

Walter winced. "What's wrong? Don't you want to be friends again?"

"Sure, why not?" Aisha watched her breath on the air and avoided looking into his eyes. "Today is the beginning of beautiful memories for us."

She held out her hand, and he clasped it in his. She curled her fingers in his palm and it felt right.

He didn't know why she took so long to respond to his friendly overture, but he liked her reserve. He wasn't used to it. Usually, females were a lot more friendly to him. Because of her laid-back attitude and her ease of being around him, he felt relaxed in her company.

She sat in silence beside him and Walter glanced at her. She was a novelty and he liked her more and more each second they sat there. He wondered what had caused her to end their friendship eight years ago. Was it something that he had said or done?

He thought about asking her and then decided against it.

Guy joined them shortly after. And then Myrtle carried hot chocolate. She had beaten and grated the chocolate herself. It had a thick and rich mouthfeel.

They chatted until it was time to get ready for church and then they walked all the way down the hill to the small building that church services were held.

It was a simple and heartfelt program, nothing like what passed for worship in Kingston and Walter found himself wishing that he never had to go back and face his church with Axel and Gia.

He liked the intimacy of the small board church and the friendliness of the country folk. The rain started pouring on the zinc roof by the time the service was close to ending. They couldn't hear the last bit of what the minister was saying.

Aisha translated for him.

"I am good at lip reading." She leaned in closer to him.

Walter could feel his ears tingling as she whispered close to them.

He was feeling inappropriately too good for the setting. He sighed in relief when the minister indicated that they would have prayer.

Walter felt a warm snug feeling when he knelt beside Aisha. It felt right, the pouring rain outside, the warmth inside and Aisha by his side with her eyes closed in prayer.

****

A couple of days later Walter was not feeling as warm and right. He had gone to the elders meeting on Tuesday night and everybody was excited about the new pastor. Axel had preached a soul-stirring message that had them excited, even the most conservative of elders, who rarely showed any emotion, Elder Marvin, was in fine form extolling the virtues of the message and the man.

Walter resisted the urge to roll his eyes. He had been enjoying the last dregs of the relaxing weekend. He tapped his pen on the boardroom table, waiting for his star-struck brethren to move on from their pastor worship.

"And his wife is a lovely woman," Elder Jimmy added.

"You mean pretty. I don't know about her attitude. She is a

little standoffish. We have never had such a pretty first lady." Elder Mary snorted. "I hope she is not given to vainglory."

"Elder Mary, come on," Elder Harding the head elder said sternly. "Why do you have to put a negative spin on things?"

"Why is it that when I am truthful, it is skewed as negative." Elder Mary shook her head. "The pastor was okay. His sermon sounded like one of them sermons you buy from the Internet. I wasn't impressed. He shouted a lot and got very emotional. It did not move me one bit. My sense of discernment says something is off."

"Lord give me strength," Elder Jimmy muttered. "Not this again."

Elder Donald chuckled. "Pastor White created his own sermons. I bet you are missing him now."

Elder Mary frowned. "I don't miss your sticky-fingered friend, Donald Green. I am just saying that if this pastor thinks he can come to our church and fool himself into thinking that much loud shouting and thumping the Bible will have us impressed he has a next think coming. We are supposed to do more than entertain. We are supposed to be people of the word. Isn't that right, Elder Walter?"

All eyes turned to him.

Walter roused himself enough to nod. "That's right."

"What is it that you know about this man, Elder Walter?" Mary asked pointedly. "I think you should speak now. Tell us."

Walter glared at Mary. She was deliberately putting him on the spot. She had not hit it off with Axel.

He inhaled and then looked around. "Yes, I do know something about Axel Parks. However, I am not willing to bring up his past at this moment. It could be that he has changed."

Besides, he was not comfortable talking about what nearly

happened to him. He had not spoken about how he felt with his brothers, and he surely wasn't going to casually discuss it with a room full of people who were not close to him.

"That's a good response, Elder Walter," Elder Harding said decisively. "Let us move on to our first item on the agenda. The homework program."

"I have gotten the commitment from over twenty-four persons to volunteer as teachers. I am going to teach Biology on a Monday. And our pastor volunteered to teach Religious Studies on a Wednesday. And our first lady who has a degree in Business Studies, volunteered to teach two classes, Tuesday and Thursday. I will be spearheading the venture."

Walter groaned. He had volunteered to teach on a Thursday. So much for avoiding Gia and Axel as much as possible.

He toyed with the idea of backing out of the program, but he had confirmed it already with Ivan. He had gotten him to promise to be in the class.

"I think it is quite exemplary that our pastor and his wife are volunteers. Maybe then we will get more people to get on board. It is for a worthy cause. The children of this church should be the brightest and sharpest in their schools, and it will save their parents paying for extra classes."

Elder Mary grunted. "I can't argue against that."

"Wonder of wonders," Elder Donald said snarkily.

Walter listened absently as they went off on one of their bickering sprees. He checked his phone surreptitiously as it vibrated on the table.

Your niece, Rosanna Wiley is here, 8 lbs, 3 oz.

It was from Preston.

Walter grinned at the phone and then got up. "Excuse me, folks, I have to run to meet a little lady at the hospital. I am an uncle again."

****

"How was Portland?"

Aisha was sitting at her desk in the staff room. She shared space with Kyra Bora, one of the morning shift teachers and a fellow Math teacher. Kyra was a pretty petite Indian girl who was friendly, talkative and well liked by everyone.

Kyra was seeing her for the first time since the weekend because she had been out sick.

Aisha smiled at Kyra. "I loved it. I mean I absolutely would go back. It rained most of the weekend, but it was still good. I hiked up to a maroon settlement; saw some giant swallowtail butterflies that are only found in that area of Jamaica. I didn't even know I was interested in butterflies before I saw them."

"Ah," Kyra said wistfully, "I wish I could get away."

"Do it. It is worth it. Plan it with rain in mind," Aisha said wistfully, "and do not go with someone who you are attracted to but is off limits. It can get romantic, watching sunrises in the morning, hiking through the rainforest and skipping puddles. And don't get me started on him helping you up inclines and then curving his hand around your waist to steady you."

Kyra frowned, "What's wrong with him, you are beautiful!"

"Beauty means nothing when you are not his type." Aisha sighed dramatically. "I am just not what he goes for."

"Ah," Kyra grimaced, "I had a boyfriend like that once. I was just not his type either. He found out when we were planning marriage."

"Yup," Aisha muttered, "life is jacked up sometimes."

"That is why you need to go out with Oliver." Kyra nodded her head to the other side of the staff room to a teacher who was sitting with his head buried in the books. "He told me he likes you."

"I am not going out with any of my colleagues," Aisha grunted. "I was already asked by John Rivers."

"Phys Ed John?" Kyra chuckled. "He is cute but crude. "

"I figured something was off," Aisha muttered, "he suggested that we skip the dating part of it… said his salary does not run to fancy dinners and that we should just find out if we are compatible between the sheets, and then we move on from there."

"John Revolta." Kyra laughed. "he comes with a standard warning label to new teachers. Oliver, on the other hand, is a sweet man."

"So why don't you go out with him?" Aisha asked doubtfully.

"I am taken, a recent development." Kyra winked at her, "or else I would be all over Oliver, trust me. The best way to get over the unavailable man in your life is to go out with other people. Oliver is much more cerebral than John, and he comes with no warning labels, trust me."

"I don't know." Aisha shrugged.

She needed some time to get her attraction and reaction to Walter Wiley under control. Oliver would not have a fair chance if she went out with him now.

She looked over at him, and their eyes met. He gave her a little wave and then went back to his book.

He looked like a pretty nice guy. He had clean-cut good-looking features and a gushing endorsement from Kyra, but she was a stickler for punishment.

She had feelings for Walter Wiley, that were pretty hard to bury.

She needed time.

Chapter Thirteen

Thursday. Walter vacillated between two options. Going to the church hall where they had the classes or calling Elder Mary and pleading a headache. He despised the thought of feeling so much like a wimp, so he went to the pool. He could exercise out any negative emotions. Except it wasn't working. His state of nervousness only fled when Aisha unexpectedly joined him.

"Hey Walter," she was wearing a bright yellow bikini that was skimpy enough to raise his heart rate.

She smiled at him unconcerned before she slipped into the water.

He was reminded afresh that he liked her. She could lift dark clouds. At least the ones in his mind and she was completely uninhibited around him.

"Hey Aisha," he responded, trying to drag his eyes from her bust line as she sluiced through the water. "Want to attend a mini party Saturday night. I am a new uncle you know. I just thought that I should celebrate it."

"That's right." Aisha grinned. "Congratulations. What's her name?"

"Rosanna." Walter grinned. "Another girl with a song title for a name just like yours."

"You know, I haven't heard that song either." Aisha swam near him and treaded water. "You need to sing it to me again."

Walter started singing it again.

Aisha looked at him fixatedly again, just like the first time he had sung it for her and he wondered if she was going to kiss him again impulsively.

He wouldn't mind. And this time there were no school rules to stop them.

And then unexpectedly Aisha burst out in tears.

Walter was not prepared for that. He stared at her helplessly. What on earth had caused that reaction?

"I er I can't come to your party Saturday night." Aisha swiped a hand across her eyes and then swam swiftly to the other end of the pool. "I can't."

"Why?" Walter asked confused.

"I need to cure myself." Aisha looked back at him accusingly.

"Cure yourself of what?" Walter asked as she grabbed her towel.

"You!" Aisha accused. "I need some distance from you."

Walter treaded the water as confused as ever. Why would she need to be cured of him, he thought things were going well between them.

The confusion was enough to keep his mind occupied until he went to church in the evening.

****

G*ia Fire.* She was standing at the church auditorium door when Walter arrived at the school. She had not changed much, was his first thought.

She was still beautiful, even more so. The years had softened her features a bit. She was curvier than he remembered, the extra weight fit her better. She had cut her very long hair, and it framed her face in a smooth straight, shiny bell.

Their eyes met before Gia looked away hurriedly to talk to Mary who had been lurking behind the door and out of Walter's line of sight.

They were in deep conversation. He cautiously approached the stairs leading up the porch area. His world had not collapsed. He was not ravaged with strange regrets. Gia was just a woman.

A woman who had been in his past. Ten years in the past. Maybe he was so calm because he had been listening to the song *Aisha* in the car and thinking about the woman.

Gia didn't have much of an impact on him at the moment.

He nodded at Gia, who was looking at him with wide-eyed wonder and Mary who nodded back while she talked.

He walked into the auditorium. The space was transformed into various spaces that could simultaneously accommodate six classes. He dearly hoped that there would not be a clash of sounds, but it seemed as if the partitions were set far enough apart to ease what would otherwise be a pretty noisy affair.

The homework program was well supported. He saw students from the community and the young people from church. They were bundled up in cliques near the soundstage part of the auditorium; quite a few of them were still in their school uniforms.

The classes were supposed to begin at six and end at eight.

He was ten minutes early.

Elder Harding walked over to him and handed him two

pieces of paper. One was a schedule of classes and the teachers and dates. The other was a syllabus.

Harding was not kidding around. He had things well organized. Walter nodded his thanks and walked toward class two which Harding said was where his class would be.

It went off without a hitch. The noise level was not as high as he had anticipated. The students were quite interested; most of them already knew the basics. And he did a couple of questions that they had for homework.

He felt good two hours later when he was finished. It was always a great feeling to volunteer. This was as close as he had come to volunteering through the years.

He mainly gave monetary gifts to charities, but he could see the merits in giving not just his money but his expertise to the younger generation.

He was basking in the glow of right-doing when he saw Gia standing beside his car.

He resisted the urge to stop and stare, so he continued walking.

"Hi Walter," Gia said when he came closer. "How are you? It's been years."

Walter nodded. "That's true. Years."

"I always wondered where you were." Gia smiled, "and then I looked you up online. I found plenty of stuff on your brothers not much on you."

"That's because I am a private person. Most of my brothers head companies or in Case's situation, a famous singer; they have to get themselves out there."

Walter shrugged and opened the car door.

"Aren't you even the least bit curious about me?" Gia asked, "What am I doing here, how I became Axel's wife?"

Walter debated saying no. It would be a lie though. He was mega curious, but he wanted to show her that he was indifferent. He turned to her fully and raised an eyebrow. "I am curious."

"You look even better than you did in uni," Gia said, "are you married? have kids?"

"No." Walter shook his head.

"Oh," Gia widened her eyes, "what on earth are you waiting for?"

"Love, a caring woman, loyalty, that kind of thing," Walter chuckled dryly, "the right person for me."

Gia nodded and her hair rippled in the half-light. "I hear you."

"You do know that I know Axel Parks don't you?" Walter blurted out before he could stop himself.

"Yes, I know, Axel tells me everything." Gia rubbed her neck. "Axel told me that he did some bad things in the past and that you were involved. He is changed now, trust me. The Lord can change anyone. He changed me."

Walter looked at her in disbelief. "How long have you two been married?"

"Four years." Gia sighed, "I was in a state. I was a high functioning addict who was hooked on a gazillion things. I had to pop pills to get me out of bed, pills to concentrate, snort some coke now and again and I did all this while holding down a job at the church."

"Church?" Walter leaned on the car and looked at Gia in mild shock.

"Yes, I ended up working at the House of Fire." Gia made a face, "Before that, I was working for a financial services company, and I tried to embezzle some funds. They caught me, told me to pay it back or go to prison. I chose to pay it back. I was blackballed in the financial district. So I had to go crawling to Daddy who was only too pleased to have me."

Walter cleared his throat. "In the church?"

"Yup. Say what you want about church people, they love a good testimony. And I had one, though it was not genuine, not at the time." Gia shrugged. "I had to work, and the church was as good a place as any to work. I had a drug and drinking habit to maintain. Can't do it without a job."

"I am not surprised about any of this," Walter said, "you were quite wild in university."

"I know." Gia mused. "I was awful to you and to so many other people. If it is any consolation, I ended up at rock bottom. One night I took a combination of drugs that sent me into a coma.

"Axel was one of my father's senior pastor's. He stopped by the next morning and found me unresponsive. If it weren't for Axel and his quick thinking, I would probably not be here now.

"It was a wake-up call. They pumped my system sent me to therapy and rehab, and I did a lot of praying. I just wanted God to fix me again, and you know what, he did. I am better today. And it is not every day somebody gets a chance to make amends. Walter, I want to say I am sorry for the way I treated you."

Walter nodded. "I got over that ages ago. I am happy that you are changed now and doing better. I guess I'll see you around."

Gia nodded and stood back. He got in his car, the song Aisha came on automatically when he started the car. He had been listening to it before class.

Gia frowned. "You like that song?"

"Love it." Walter grinned. "Always did."

"I have a cousin named Aisha." Gia volunteered, "I haven't seen her in years."

Walter couldn't resist saying. "Aisha and I were very good

friends in university, and ironically she is now my neighbor."

Gia frowned. "Really? This world is pretty small isn't it?"

"I say that all the time." Walter started to back out of the parking space when a black SUV stopped too close behind him for him to maneuver pass it comfortably.

The window wound down slowly, and Axel pushed out his head. "Is that Walter Wiley?"

Walter would recognize Axel's voice anywhere.

Axel got out of his car and came over to Walter's. Making a show of kissing Gia on the cheek and then turning to Walter dramatically.

"How are you, Walter?"

"I am surprisingly well, considering that you are the pastor of this church." Walter tried to keep the hostility from his voice. The truth was, Axel looked the same. He had hardly aged.

"I go where the Lord leads," Axel said smoothly.

He sounded even more pastorly than before.

"You still watch porn and try to drug and rape boys?" Walter asked cutting through the politeness.

Axel blanched and Gia gasped.

"That's uncalled for, Walter," Gia whispered, "I told you it is all in the past."

"And I am telling you," Walter said to Axel, "that I have my eye on you. If you so much as look cross-eyed at a boy in this church, I am going to make sure that you never work again. You see, I am all grown up now, and I can spot grooming from a mile away. Just try it, and I'll take you down."

Then he looked at Gia balefully, "I hope for your sake that your husband has sorted out his little proclivities."

"Now Walter, this is uncalled for," Axel sputtered. "What happened, happened ages ago. I was a young pastor. I had issues. Haven't you done things in your past that you have regretted?"

"Yes," Walter said bitingly, "your wife, Gia, for close to a year. I regretted that."

"I was hoping for a cordial relationship at least," Axel said piously ignoring his dig about Gia.

"I know what you tried to do to me," Walter snarled, "cordial is a tall ask. We can forgive but forgetting is another thing. Why on earth are the two of you in Jamaica anyway?"

"Change of environment," Gia said quickly. "We needed a change."

Walter narrowed his eyes at them. They looked like they were hiding something.

He didn't trust them as far as he could throw them. He felt himself getting more upset than he should. He struggled for calm and inclined his head. "Can you please move your vehicle Pastor Axel?"

He sneered when he said 'pastor.'

Axel nodded jerkily.

He looked a tad guilty to Walter's suspicious eyes, but he hurriedly got in his car and moved it so that he could pass.

Walter left with the feeling that something was amiss with the couple. Their claims of change he wasn't buying it.

Walter called Saint who was probably asleep. London time was six hours ahead.

Saint answered the phone groggily. "Walter this had better be good. I just went to bed."

"How is it going?" Walter asked.

"Good," Saint mumbled. "I miss home though. I am never going to get used to the weather. What's up?"

"Axel Parks," Walter said, "and Gia Fire Parks his wife."

"Say again?" Saint sounded alert. "Axel Parks is the reason I went into the investigation business, after what he did to you."

"He is now our church pastor." Walter sighed. "I don't trust that he is changed. I guess I am a suspicious person by nature..."

"Say no more." Saint sounded like he was salivating. "If he or Gia Fire...why does that name sound familiar?"

"The girl from university." Walter grimaced. "The one who almost destroyed my life."

"Even better," Saint said, "if they are not on the up and up, I will find out."

"Thanks, bro," Walter said gratefully. "Go back to sleep."

"Can't sleep now," Saint said ruefully, "I have things to do."

Chapter Fourteen

Aisha woke up on Friday morning to find a gift box on her doorstep. It contained a CD with her name on it and a note with the song lyrics that Walter was telling her about. She listened to the song while she drove to work and had the strangest urge to cry like she did yesterday while Walter sang it to her.

Why on earth was he so perfect and yet so wrong?

It was not fair.

She got a call from her mother while she was in the school parking lot smoothing down the front of her hair. It was stubbornly resisting the gel that she had applied. She loved her hair, but sometimes she wished it were more like her mother's and aunts. They had silky curls that were easy to manage.

She remembered how Gia would tease her about her coarser hair and call it ugly. That's why she had processed it in the first place but through the years she had grown to love it. She had started appreciating that it was not ugly. It was big, luscious, thick and gravity-defying and she and her hair were now at peace.

"Honey," her mother said after the pleasantries. "I got a call from Gia."

Aisha groaned. "I wondered when she would reach out."

"I invited her and her husband to the house tonight," Grace said hurriedly. "Please say you'll come. She specifically asked for you to be there."

Aisha made a face at the phone. "I am not interested."

"She is family, Aisha," Her mother said, a plea in her voice. "I have never understood why you two have never gotten along."

"What is there to understand?" Aisha asked incredulously. "Gia used to blame me for every mishap that she got into and then watch gleefully as I took the punishment. Not to mention that she called me ugly and fat every chance she got. I grew up thinking that I was hideous and almost developed an eating disorder because of Gia. Mom, some relatives are too toxic to associate with, Gia is one of them."

Grace sighed. "Oh come on, Aisha. Gia is changed now. She is a Christian and married to a pastor."

"Which means nothing." Aisha snorted cynically. "Christianity is not church going. I would have to see her in action before I would conclude that she has changed."

Her mother pounced on the last statement. "So come reacquaint yourself with her, and you'll see."

Aisha had gotten herself into that one. She sighed heavily down the phone. "Will Mark be there?"

"Yes but Mark is on medication to lower his stress levels. He has been well for months now," Grace said. "He even has a girlfriend and is talking about moving out."

"If you are sure," Aisha sighed, she couldn't even use

Mark as an excuse. "I'll be there then. Say, mom, how did you come up with my name?"

Grace laughed. "Aisha Amara Fire? Which one of them?"

"Aisha," She said impatiently.

"When we were living in Ethiopia, there was a pretty little girl who lived in the house beside us. I liked the name. I thought that when I had my own pretty little girl, I'd name her Aisha."

"Oh," Aisha sighed, "I thought you got it from the song."

"Which song?" Grace asked.

Aisha took a few moments to explain and then she hung up the phone and scowled at her reflection in the car mirror. She disliked going to her mother's house, because of her stepbrother Mark and now she had to deal with Gia as well. It was too much.

But her suddenly busy, emotional life was about to get busier. She met Oliver in the staff room who handed her a note. *Would you like to go out on Saturday night?*

No, she wouldn't like to go out on Saturday night.

She sat at her desk and searched for her Teacher's Diary. All the while wondering how she was going to shake Walter Wiley from her mind and let Oliver down gently.

****

Friday night dinner. Aisha parked beside her stepfather's Audi Q5. The townhouse was in a gated community not unlike the one where the Wiley's lived. She rarely visited when Mark was there and only when he was functional and stress-free.

Mark had a recurring delusion that he was living on the wrong earth. He had elaborate theories that historical events were not the same on the earth that he was coming from and that his life events were much different. In that state of delusion, he was always looking for a way to get back to his world.

To his credit, his descriptions of the alternate world were always consistent, and he even had different names for things and could speak fluent Spanish. It was fun to question him as to what was happening in his alternate earth because it was nothing like the present one.

His alternate earth had a different beginning. Eve had never eaten the fruit and so Adam and Eve had passed that test with flying colors. Sin had entered the world at some later date by one of Eve's descendants.

According to Mark, there had been no flood. Therefore there were no islands. The earth was not divided up into continents and had the same temperature across the globe. The land that is now called North America was called Espacio Verde in the other earth. Apparently, the language that everyone spoke was Spanish.

She first spent the summer at the house when she was thirteen. Big, affable, sweet, delusional Mark hit her on the head with an iron skillet, on her first day there claiming she was an intruder and working for a race of people called the Grim Ones or Sombrios. Luckily, her mother had been around to stop him before he could hit her again.

The second time she was sixteen, sleeping in the guest room when Mark had tried to smother her with a pillow. Apparently, she was again spying on him for the Sombrios and should be stopped.

The irony of the whole thing was that he was a perfectly normal guy when he wasn't trying to kill people. He never remembered any of his mental lapses and was usually remorseful when he heard what he did.

Aisha rang the front doorbell, and Mark answered the door

with a wide smile on his face.

"Sis! I never see enough of you."

And for a good reason, Aisha thought before smiling.

"Bro! Whats up with you?"

"Lots of things." Mark grinned widely. "I am so in love and happy I could burst."

Aisha grinned back at him. It was good to see him so happy.

"You should try it," Mark said shrugging into a black suede jacket.

"Try what?" Aisha asked.

"Love. It is more effective than my psychosis pills," Mark said wryly.

"I love someone, I have loved him for years." Aisha shrugged. "It is making me less than happy."

"Are you certain it is love?" Mark asked, "because love is amazing! I feel amazing! And I am on my way out to spend some time with her. Have a good time at supper."

Aisha nodded and watched him go through the door. She hoped that he would remember that his new love was in this earth. Maybe at least Mark would be inclined to stick around more in this reality.

Gia and her husband were already in the kitchen, sitting at the island and chatting to Grace like they were long lost, old friends.

"Oh hey, Aisha," Gia said as soon as she saw her. She got up to hug her.

Aisha hugged her back reluctantly. Smiled at her husband Axel after the introductions and wondered in silent desperation why she had agreed to come. There were too many scar tissues on her emotions that Gia was personally responsible for. She would never be chummy with Gia.

It was never going to happen.

Grace was almost as delusional as Mark if she thought that

she and Gia could play happy family.

Gia was her usual superficial bubbly self, Aisha thought resentfully as she steered the conversation to talk about herself of course. Her charity work, her missionary travels, her metamorphosis into Mother Theresa.

Her husband was smiling and nodding and looking at her as if the sun rose and set on her. It was gag worthy.

"So what have you been up to, Aisha?" Gia finally asked.

"Nothing as saintly as you." Aisha smiled dryly. "Just started a new job."

"And you live in Kingston now," Gia stated the obvious. "I must visit. We can hang out like old times."

Aisha started coughing. Grace had to give her a glass of water and a stern look.

Aisha shook her head vigorously before answering, "I have no time to hang out."

"But teachers have weekends and summers, and every holiday there is to have in this country." Gia smiled at her sweetly. "I am sure you can find time to spend with your cousin."

"First of all," Aisha glared at Gia, "we deserve every single holiday that there is. Teachers have to contend with a lot of stress at school."

"Woah, don't be defensive," Gia said still with that phony I want to be friends look, "I just thought that we could reconnect."

Aisha shrugged non-comittally.

"She can spare a weekend or so," Grace said helpfully. "She spent last weekend in Portland with her new friends."

"Portland," Axel looked at her with interest. "I was once assigned to Portland. As a young pastor. Which side did you go to?"

"The Upper Rio Grande Valleys." Aisha latched on to the

chance to stop talking about hanging with Gia. "It was rustic and green and gorgeous and rained most of the weekend but I had fun. Very lovely place."

"It is lovely," Axel said wistfully, "I sometimes wish I had stayed there longer. I loved the Willow Tree church."

"Willow Tree," Aisha murmured, "that was the Wiley brother's old church."

"Yes. You know the Wiley brothers?" Axel asked cautiously.

"Yes, they are my neighbors for the time being. I went to Portland with Walter and Guy. I asked Walter to let me go along because I had never been to Portland."

Axel nodded and then looked away as if he regretted bringing it up.

Aisha was almost sorry when her stepfather walked into the room. She wanted to pursue why Axel had that scared look on his face but when Anton Bulldozer King entered the room, everything else stopped.

He was a blustery fellow, full-bodied, and tall. He towered over everybody in height and personality.

Not even Gia could beat him when it came to putting the spotlight on himself. His nickname was Bulldozer, Bull for short. His grandchildren called him Grandpa Bully, his nieces and nephews called him Uncle Bully. Aisha called him Dad. He was the closest she had to one.

As usual, he enveloped her in a bear hug and gave her a sound kiss on her forehead. Had a wrestling handshake with Axel, declared him soft, ruffled Gia's perfectly coiffed hair and called her little lady and then danced his wife around the kitchen and proceeded to give her an x-rated kiss before he sat down to supper.

It turned out to be a good night. As usual Bull knew how to keep a room entertained and he didn't mind poking at himself, his family members or friends. He even had Axel relaxed around him and cracking a joke or two himself.

For once Gia was mostly quiet.

"I must come to your church, Axel," Bull said, "I like you. I want to hear you preach."

"If you are going to anybody's church it's mine." Grace chipped in. "You like him, but you love me."

"There is that." Bull laughed. "I go to Grace's church first, but I am afraid of them, they look at me and see dollar signs."

Grace got up and brought a cherry crumble to the table with bowls of vanilla ice cream.

"Aisha's favorite," she announced and gave Aisha a wink.

Aisha smiled, and then her eyes met Gia's, and she saw what looked like displeasure pass over her cousin's face.

Gia still liked to be the center of attention. Aisha almost laughed out loud. In the past, if her or Gia's parents showed Aisha the slightest bit of concern or favor, it was enough to make Gia go off the rails.

If that fleeting look was anything to go by, Gia was still crazily possessive and unnaturally jealous of her.

It was only later in college after Aisha got a list of disorders to study for a psychology course that she realized that Gia had narcissistic personality disorder. She literally had all the traits of the disorder—a lack of empathy, a need for admiration, arrogance, self-centered, manipulative, and demanding.

Indeed she was the poster child for NPD. Aisha excused herself and went to the guest bathroom. When she got out, Gia was standing at the door.

"Hey," Gia smiled, "I decided that I wanted to go too."

Aisha nodded. "Okay."

"Say," Gia paused at the door. "I desperately wanted to ask you about Walter Wiley."

"What about him?" Aisha stopped in her tracks.

"What is it like dating a gay guy?" Gia asked widening her eyes for emphasis.

"I don't know." Aisha said, "Walter and I are not dating. We are just hanging out."

"Ah," Gia nodded, "like old times, huh. I was shocked when I heard you two mentioned together. I hoped you remembered that I told you he was gay."

Aisha gritted her teeth angrily. "Yes, I remember."

"Good," Gia said smiling. "I need your number. I must visit with you, Aisha. I am excited about us reconnecting."

"Over my dead body," Aisha muttered as she walked away.

Chapter Fifteen

Aisha was avoiding him. Walter was busy but not too busy to notice that she disappeared whenever he entered the gym or drove into the driveway. He visited with Shawn to play with Courtney at the pool two weeks after the puzzling event with Aisha.

Shawn was alone with the toddler, Jordan was still at work.

"Hey," Shawn greeted him brightly when he knocked on the door. "You are just the man I wanted to see. Your niece's birthday party is coming up, and I told Jordan that I would plan the party. That I would not impose on you because you have a lot going on. Can you believe she is going to be one?"

Walter looked around the house, "where is she?"

"On the patio with our visitor, Aisha."

"Great girl by the way," Shawn lowered her voice, "why on earth haven't you made a move yet?"

"Because she is avoiding me," Walter whispered. "I have no idea why."

Shawn nodded, "I'll find out for you my favorite brother-in-law."

"Liar. I am not your favorite. I heard you telling Case that he was your favorite," Walter snorted. "What is it that you want me to do for this party?"

"I am serious, you are my favorite brother-in-law today," Shawn grinned at him. "I was extolling your virtues to Aisha. I told her that you secretly planned my wedding. I told her you were an excellent cook, you clean up after yourself, that you are a social butterfly but notoriously private when it comes to your family and friends. That you are humble and kind and sweet and you love children."

"Good work." Walter headed to the patio.

"It's the truth." Shawn smiled. "I am going to pop over to Sheryl's for a while. Aisha won't want to abandon the baby she and Courtney have a mutual admiration thing going on. Pretend as if you have to wait until I get back."

"Thanks." Walter smiled at her.

Aisha was playing peek-a-boo with Courtney who was giggling and bouncing on her lap.

"Hey, motherhood looks good on you."

Aisha glanced at him, "I know right. I love kids. I especially love them at this cuddly baby stage."

Courtney chortled when she saw him and held out her hands to him, forgetting Aisha.

Aisha groaned, "What is it with you and girls. They flock to you like you have a homing device."

Walter took Courtney from Aisha and laughed.

"This particular girl loves her uncle Walter to pieces because he has been talking to her since she was in her mommy's belly."

Courtney cuddled up to him like a velcro baby snuggling herself on his neck a look of contentment on her face.

"So what's up, Aisha Fire? Why are you avoiding me?" Walter raised an eyebrow. "Curious minds want to know."

Aisha shifted uncomfortably in the patio chair and avoided his stare. She had on very short shorts and a tank top with the words: *I am sexy, and I know it.*

Walter nodded imperceptibly. *That is very true.* She was in her signature hairstyle, but the curly puff seemed a lot less neat than usual. She didn't have on makeup, and her lips were bare and red. She was slim and had curves in all the right places. She didn't look much older than when they were in college.

He resisted the urge to walk right over to her and shake out whatever it is was that she was hiding from him. Aisha was too secretive for her own good.

"Okay, tell me this," Walter sat across from her with Courtney still cuddled in his arms. "Why did you stop talking to me eight years ago?"

Aisha sighed. "You want the truth?"

"Of course," Walter narrowed his gaze at her.

"I liked you...a lot." Aisha groaned, "you have no idea how much. I was smitten, besotted, enchanted, enraptured, captivated...did I say besotted?"

Walter leaned forward. "Say that again."

"All of it? I was searching for synonyms that could describe my craziness."

"Then why did you stop talking to me. I wrote you letters." Walter grimaced, "I loved our friendship. I thought we had something special."

"Me too." Aisha nodded, "and then I spoke to Gia who swore me to secrecy, and she told me about you."

Walter groaned. "Gia told you. Everything?"

"Yes, she did." Aisha grimaced, "I was shattered. I had a very miserable time in Europe. I was not much fun to be around. You should see the pictures; all my smiles were forced."

"Did Gia go into details about what happened? If you had told me about what she said, we could have had that conversation. Instead, you cut me off. That hurt, you know."

"I know." Aisha sighed, "It was probably an immature way to handle the news, but I was shell-shocked."

Walter sighed. "She told you about the drugs, the sex, the orgies, the parties?"

"No," Aisha gasped looking at him like he had suddenly morphed into a monster. "She didn't tell me any of that."

Walter could slap himself when he looked at the horror in her eyes. *So what exactly did Gia tell her that had shocked her into not speaking to him? Was it that stupid sex tape?*

"It was ten years ago. I have been clean living ever since!" Walter defended himself.

Aisha covered her face. And there was silence for what seemed like forever. She finally peeked at him through her fingers. "Okay."

"So stop avoiding me." Walter couldn't stop the plea in his voice. "I like the fact that you are here now as my neighbor, we could be friends again. Go on adventures together. Wasn't Uncle Micky's place fun?"

Aisha looked at him for a long time before answering. "Yes, it was fun and romantic. The thing is, I can't handle stuff like that with you. I get emotionally involved; I start thinking about us as a couple..."

"And what is so wrong about that?" Water shifted Courtney to his other arm. She had fallen asleep on him and was making snuffling sounds.

"I can't pretend like your past didn't happen, and everything is just honky dory, and you are...never mind."

Walter sighed. "I should have told you and not allow Gia

to do it. The fact is, after the business with the sex tape."

Aisha gasped. "Sex tape?"

"So you didn't know about that?" Walter groaned. "It wasn't even a sex tape as such, I mean we were in costume, and there was a whip involved, a little role-playing, I was supposed to be a..."

Aisha held up her hand. "I don't want to hear details. You know what, I'll stop avoiding you, I need some time to process all of this."

Walter frowned, "Just remember that this was years ago, almost a decade."

Aisha nodded. "Yep. I'll remember."

"And this has nothing to do with you and me, now." Walter reiterated.

Aisha nodded doubtfully.

"So this weekend, we can go to Guy's place in the hills? It's strawberry season."

Shawn chose that time to return home. She put Courtney down for a nap, and the conversation moved from personal topics but why was it that Walter still felt uneasy?

Aisha was refusing to look at him directly, and she had not said yes to his weekend away proposal.

****

Aisha had to escape Walter Wiley at least for a while. Unfortunately, it was not to be for that weekend. Guy had called her shortly after Walter had extended his invitation and had practically begged her to come and sample his new varieties of strawberries and to see his farm.

She had hated to say no. She was living in Guy's townhouse rent-free. He had said yes to putting her up when he could have ignored her. The least she could do was show interest in his strawberry farm. And normally she would be, she loved strawberries, she loved strawberry flavored everything.

She even loved Coldplay's song, Strawberry Swing, even though it had nothing to do with strawberries. She turned up the music while she was driving from work, stuck in Friday traffic. Compounding the horrendously slow moving traffic was the rain.

She wound up her window and sang along to the song. She repeated the line, *"now the sky could be blue, I don't mind, without you, it's a waste of time."*

Of course, she thought of Walter when she sang the verse and of course she had to castigate herself for her stupidity and of course it didn't matter.

After their conversation on Wednesday, she had looked up on the Internet, how to kill sexual attraction.

One article recommended drugs, exhaustion, and avoidance. She had read the column with a certain amount of incredulity.

She was not going to take drugs or physically exert herself above the norm, so avoiding the object of her affection would have to do because being around Walter was torture.

Barbarous and excruciating torture.

She had done nothing to deserve this. Her brain chemicals or body make up was out of whack.

She heard that the man was involved in all sorts of debauchery and she still liked him. It just was not fair. She should be so horrified by the things he told her she couldn't bear to look at him, but alas, it wasn't working.

She crawled a little toward the intersection when the traffic eased up a bit, and her phone started ringing. She answered it without looking at the call display. It was a testament to her frame of mind because she always checked who was calling before answering. She didn't like surprises.

And of course, she was unpleasantly surprised.

"Hello Aisha," Gia said cheerily.

Aisha grunted. "Hey."

"It has been weeks, and I did promise to keep in touch, didn't I?"

"And I did say I didn't care if you did," Aisha replied trying to keep the grumpiness from her voice.

"Oh well," Gia brushed away her lack of enthusiasm. "Why don't you show up at church tomorrow and we can have a potluck after."

"No can do, I am going away for the weekend." Aisha was happy that she could truthfully say that.

"Where?" Gia asked sharply.

"To a strawberry farm. It sounds heavenly the way that Guy describes it."

"Guy?" Gia asked, "as in Guy Wiley?"

"Yes, his place," Aisha said.

"So you live in his house, and you are spending weekends with him?" Gia laughed, "and here I thought that you were interested in Walter. You go girl. I am happy for you. When is the wedding?"

"Wedding?" Aisha growled. "There is no wedding. Guy and I are just friends. We kept in touch sporadically through the years, and the other day when I needed help, I contacted him."

"Oh," Gia sounded solemn again. "I guess I thought differently."

"I guess you did." Aisha hung up without saying goodbye and then felt petty after that.

She was the mean girl in their current relationship, Gia was trying to reach out, even pretending to be happy for her and she was not trying to meet her halfway. Maybe it was time to give up the grudge.

She turned the radio up as she got stuck in another line of traffic.

Chapter Sixteen

"You owe me." Guy was saying in Walter's ear as he packed the car for the weekend. The rain had eased up a bit, and he wanted to take advantage of the lull. "I made Aisha feel so guilty for not wanting to see my farm. I feel kind of bad about how I did it."

"I owe you nothing." Walter grunted. "It is your brotherly duty to ensure that I am happy. Aisha makes me happy, and she says she wants an old-fashioned courting, so I am giving it to her."

Guy chuckled. "I guess it is also my brotherly duty to be scarce this weekend."

"You are a genius. Mensa knew what they were about when they certified you."

Guy laughed. "My being scarce has nothing to do with intelligence but merely common sense. I hope you use yours and win Aisha. I have lots of strawberry and chocolate to help you out."

Walter laughed and hung up the phone. It rang shortly after that and he answered.

"Hey Walter, it's Gia."

Gia has my number? Walter frowned.

"I thought that in the spirit of good Christian reconciliation that you could come to a potluck with us tomorrow."

"No thank, you Gia," Walter said slamming the car door, "I am going away for the weekend."

"At Guy's farm?" Gia asked.

"How do you know that?" Walter asked suspiciously.

"I spoke with Aisha. She said she was going away too after I extended an invitation to her. Are you two in a relationship?"

"That's none of your business." Walter leaned on the car. "We are not friends, Gia. Please don't call my phone again."

Gia was silent for a while and when she spoke her voice was wounded. "Walter, please don't be rude. I invited all the elders and their spouses, and you are an elder, hence the call. As for my cousin, I thought it would be nice to invite her as well, but she told me she was going away for the weekend.

"Do not read anything into this invite. I am just being polite. I realize though that it will take a while for us to move past our past but it can be done. I am determined that it should be done.

"Christians are not supposed to be cold to each other. Surely we are more mature than that with nearly three decades under our belt and a lot of living since we last saw each other."

Walter sighed down the phone. It was true. He was acting immature. He had been reacting badly to Gia and Axel ever since they showed up. It was time to stop. Hadn't he told Aisha emphatically that the past was past.

He cleared his throat. "I am sorry. You are right. I am acting immature; I will address that in our future dealings."

****

They started the weekend with a bang. Aisha had psyched up herself into thinking that she could be just friends with Walter. She was doing a pretty good job at pretending until she forgot the pretense and was laughing at Walter's jokes and singing along to his father's 50's CD.

"I found a bunch of fifties CDs in his things at the house in Portland," Walter said. "I think that my father had given them to his father as a present or something. One summer I was home and decided to play them, and then I thought, I love this era in music."

"Me too." Aisha nodded along to The Everly Brother's, All I Have to Do is Dream. Ironically, she was dreaming her life away with Walter. She squashed the thought away and smiled at him.

"You don't talk about your father much."

"I didn't know him well." Walter shrugged. "I had the misfortune of being the child of the wife he didn't love. And my mother didn't want him to be too close to us."

"Ah," Aisha murmured, "do you resent the brothers who did get to know him?"

"No." Walter glanced at her, "that would be crazy, and the only two brothers who qualified as closest to our father would be Jordan and Guy. They are the brothers that I feel the closest to."

"I noticed." Aisha smiled. "You know I have a brother and a sister, right? My father's children, both of them older. They weren't close to my dad, and I grew up not knowing them."

"That could have easily happened to us." Walter slowed down as the rain seemed as though it was coming down in sheets.

"I love being in a car, warm and dry listening to oldies while the rain pours outside," Aisha said wistfully.

Walter looked over at her and gave her an intense stare before remarking.

"There is a certain charm to it, especially when you are with somebody you are er...comfortable with."

Aisha inhaled raggedly, was it only her that felt the tension between them? She had never felt this way about a man before so she had no real reference. The only thing she could compare it to was their time in university, and even then the magnetism was not as strong. It was as if it had gone up a hundredfold and then some. She could feel the hair on her arms rising, her skin prickled with it. She licked her lips because they were suddenly dry.

With difficulty, she dragged her eyes from Walter's. She was not feeling comfortable in any way shape or form.

She was feeling hot and bothered and as uncomfortable as it was possible to be with them locked up in an intimate setting.

She tried to drag her mind from her attraction and changed the topic. "Talk to me about when you were a boy."

Tell me stories. Distract me. Aisha added to herself desperately. She needed to pray about this madness that was taking over her body. If she could react this way with the husband she knew God was providing for her, they would never get up to go to work.

Walter stopped in a long line of traffic with a stop sign that seemed a mile ahead.

"Aisha," his voice was husky, "what's going in that mind of yours?"

Aisha looked at him shyly. "I was just wondering what it would be like to kiss you." *Did that come out of my mouth? This was Walter. Where was my filter? How could I just...*

Walter pulled his seat belt and turned to her. His mouth swooped down on hers before she could ask him what he was doing.

His lips were soft and tasted slightly like peppermint. They explored hers tentatively at first, and then they became more demanding. She was the one who deepened the kiss. She felt as if she could devour him live. She wanted Walter Wiley, and all her inhibitions were down.

Her fingers crept up involuntarily to draw him closer, and the kiss went on until they heard the blare of horns around them.

Only then did Walter straighten up and started the car.

"That's what it's like," he smiled at her.

She turned dazed and uncomprehending eyes to his. "Well... er...I didn't know that all I had to do was ask."

****

Guy's place was amazing Aisha had to admit when they eventually got there late in the evening. She was feeling a sense of being in a dreamland. She had pinched her self, and it had hurt. So she was confidently sure that this whole thing was real, but it didn't have to be, maybe she had the same sense of delusion that her stepbrother Mark had.

Maybe, she had somehow slipped into an alternate universe. If so she did not want to go back to the real one. She could still feel the imprint of Walter's lips on hers.

The sweet scent of strawberry hit her when they reached the entrance to Guy's property, and she understood why when they drove up the hill to his place. Strawberries bordered the driveway on three tiers of white fences. In the car's light, she could see their red shapes hanging down on what looked like a white fence.

"Is this the farm?" She whispered.

Walter laughed. "This is Guy's version of a flower garden. He doesn't like to waste space on any plant that is not usable or saleable. His greenhouses are spread out over three acres. He will show you those in the light of day."

They drove up to the farmhouse which looked nothing like any farmhouse she had envisioned. It was a mansion; the front was covered in cut stone. Some arches extended around the place.

She figured there would be a view in the day.

Two lychee trees stood like sentries at the entry. The air was cool. Much cooler than she had been prepared for after the heat of Kingston.

Guy's housekeeper, Catherine greeted them at the door. She was a plump, matronly woman who had an accent Aisha could not place. She hugged Walter and shook her hand warmly.

"Guy is in his suite," he said he would be freshening up for dinner in anticipation of your arrival. "Let me allow you both to do the same."

Inside the house was an open plan space with wooden beams in the ceiling—cut stone lined one wall and the fireplace.

It was the same color as the stones outside.

Walter saw her fascination with the stonewall.

"Most of the material in here came from the land," Walter said helpfully. "The trees, the stones, Guy doesn't waste a thing."

The space was beautiful and homely even though it was large.

"And here I was feeling guilty for staying at his townhouse," Aisha whispered. "This is gorg. I wouldn't leave it not for a day."

Walter laughed. "Don't feel guilty. Along with this place and the townhouse, Guy owns a beachside cottage in Portland and a recently acquired mango farm in St. Ann with a house attached. And I don't doubt that Uncle Micky's place will eventually belong to him."

"Wow," Aisha whispered after Catherine showed her to a guest suite. It had a hardwood floor, a four poster bed and a patio with two flower pots filled with strawberry plants—big red juicy looking strawberries were spilling over the sides. She picked one to taste it.

She then went back inside and stared at her reflection in the floor to ceiling mirror. It was attached to what she assumed was a walk-in closet. Why couldn't she have fallen for this brother? Things would have been less complicated.

Instead, she had fallen for the gay one, who had given her the best kiss of her life. She touched her lips and lay back on the bed.

For goodness sakes, why had he kissed her? He just complicated things between them in the worst possible way. She was not going to be thinking friends after this. No way.

Chapter Seventeen

The weekend at Guy's place was just the rejuvenator that Walter needed. It rained, so they mostly stayed inside, Guy couldn't remain as scarce as he had said he would. They played pool, Aisha was a formidable opponent. She had him and Guy scrambling to try to beat her. It was a friendly and laid back outing filled with strawberries and chocolate and lovely views in the day.

That was why two weekends later he was sitting in their weekly elder's meeting staring at their special guest, Pastor Axel Parks and struggling to hold on to the calm and light feeling of the weekend.

He knew that he would have meetings like this with Axel either spearheading it or being a special guest.

He had skipped the board meeting that Axel hosted last week and would have avoided this one if Harding had not sprung the special guest announcement right when he had walked in and sat down. He knew he could not avoid Axel forever, but he was willing to give it a try.

One thing was for sure. If the way he was grinding his teeth after everything Axel said was any indication of their future meetings, this one would be the first and the last.

He was the odd man out in his feelings. Of the twelve elders sitting in the room, he was the only one not besotted with the not so new pastor. He was there for five weeks, and already he was well liked.

Just like he and his brothers had liked him in the past. Axel had always been a charming, friendly person. What was not to like?

Even Mary, the forever skeptic was lapping up what he was saying with attentiveness. She had stopped complaining that he got his sermons from the internet and she was nodding along to whatever Axel said.

Walter tuned in reluctantly. He couldn't be a leader in the church and not know what was going on.

Maybe he should resign, take a back seat, wait until Gia and Axel left or better yet go to church with Aisha. She had started visiting her mother's church, though their worship services were a little bit too lively for him.

"Elder Walter, what do you think?"

Walter looked up from doodling Aisha's name on the paper with the minutes of the previous meeting and stared in Axel's general direction.

"I didn't hear a word you said," Walter admitted honestly.

Axel cleared his throat, a hint of discomfort about him. "Well then, Elder Mary what do you think?"

"I think it is a splendid idea," Mary said, "if Elder Walter had been listening I am sure he would think so too. You know he loves working with young people. So many of them don't have proper role models. I am volunteering Ivan to be the first person to sign up."

"I am in," Elder Harding said, "It should be fun. My wife is constantly at me to go to the gym. Walter, maybe you can have your brother's join, I know Jordan would not mind a church football and cricket league. We haven't been seeing him in a while. And though Preston is attending our sister church over in New Kingston, I am sure that this would be a fun thing for him and Pete to do."

So they were talking about football.

He had grave suspicions as to why Axel wanted to surround himself with boys. He didn't trust him. He couldn't trust him.

He narrowed his eyes and looked at Axel. "I don't know about that."

"Come on Walter. You are a cricket fiend. You love the sport!" Harding glared at him. "You proposed this very idea a couple of years ago when we had the young people loitering after church having nothing to do. When Pastor Axel suggested this, you were the first person that came to mind."

Count me out. Walter wanted to growl. *I am not going to be involved with anything Axel Parks has planned.*

But then the thought came to him that maybe he should stick around to keep a close eye on Axel and how he interacted with the boys.

"Okay," he said reluctantly, "count me in."

"And me too," Elder Jimmy said, "I think some exercise would do me good."

"Sunday mornings at five-thirty," Axel grinned, "rain or shine. Gentlemen this will boost the morale of our young men much more than you know. Sports is a unifier, I saw it in my old church, and I think it would be perfect here."

****

Walter drove into the complex and saw a strange car parked beside Aisha's. He glanced at his watch, it was after eight, not particularly late. She could have visitors, why did he feel overly anxious?

He parked in his driveway and contemplated going over under some false pretext to see who she had for company. He felt like one part stalker and one part jealous boyfriend. He was more invested in Aisha than he had originally thought and he wasn't even her boyfriend.

Maybe it was the kiss. He had wanted to kiss her. He had been desperate with it and then she had asked. He did it, and his dormant libido was now back in full force. As far as he was concerned, that kiss meant that they were no longer just friends.

He waited to see who her night visitor was. He sat in his car for a full forty minutes, his eyes trained on the door and then a man came out of the house. A tall guy, who looked very much like the actor Orlando Jones, he had to do a double take. He was dressed semi-formally, his long sleeve shirt was rolled up to his elbows.

When he drove out of the complex, Walter got out of his car and without hesitation knocked on Aisha's door.

She opened it, "You forgot your glasses!"

Walter shook his head, "no, I did not."

"Oh, Walter." Aisha smiled. "What's up?"

"Nothing." Walter folded his arms and leaned on the door. "Just wanted to see you."

Aisha mimicked his pose. "Well, here I am."

He looked her over. She was dressed in a grey tracksuit. Not exactly seductive material for the guy that just left.

"Whose glasses is that?" He asked feigning a casualty that he wasn't feeling.

"Kwame Blunt, a math teacher at my school who I am

tutoring," Aisha answered just as casually. "He is doing his masters and needed help."

"Okay," Walter nodded, "good. You want to come over and tell me about your day? I need a distraction."

"Let's go to the gym instead." Aisha twisted her neck from side to side. "I am dressed for it. I could let off some steam, and then we can talk about my day and yours."

"Good idea. What happened to get you so wound up?" Walter asked.

"I taught extra classes to the slow learners, filled in for a teacher. Enough said." Aisha grimaced. "Sometimes, I wish I taught kindergarten or lectured at university."

Walter grinned.

"Or at least a subject that was well liked, a very few of my students like mathematics it is disheartening. Enough about me. What's up with you?"

"I had elders meeting. The pastor was there. He is planning some sporting event involving young boys. I am not particularly pleased."

"Why not?" Aisha asked.

"So Gia didn't tell you that?" Walter looked at Aisha suspiciously, "I thought that was it."

"What are you talking about?" Aisha asked.

"The reason why you stopped talking to me eight years ago." Walter sighed. "Give me five minutes, I have to change, and then I'll tell you about Axel."

****

The gym was empty when they got there a few minutes to nine. Aisha headed for the treadmill, and he got on the one beside her.

"Tell me about Axel," she said punching in a walking

pace on the treadmill. "He seemed nice when we were at my mom's for dinner. Come to think of it. He did mention that he knew you and your brothers when you were in Portland."

"Oh, he did," Walter smirked. "He rented from us, at the side of our house. And he was a nice enough person. We watched movies together. He loved African movies and cricket matches. And he had a big screen television.

"We were over there a lot. And then one day, he drugged me, and tried to rape me."

Aisha's gasp could be heard above the whirring of the treadmill. She stopped it and turned to Walter. "Say what?"

"My brother's found me before he could do the deed. I still remember him kissing me before I passed out."

"So why isn't he in jail?" Aisha growled. "Why isn't he locked up somewhere dark?"

"Because he didn't actually do it and he had some stupid story," Walter glanced at Aisha. "They fired him from the church, and he went elsewhere. And now he is back."

"Oh my word," Aisha muttered. "Does Gia know about what happened?"

"Yep." Walter nodded. "They both have skeletons in their closet, which they have made peace with. And they seem to be happy but what gives me pause is Axel and these boys. I am not going to be able to trust him ever."

"I wouldn't either," Aisha shook her head. "My goodness. It must have been horrible for you."

"Yes." Walter shrugged, "but I got over it. I had my grand rebellion where I acted out."

"The drugs and orgies?" Aisha looked at him sorrowfully.

"Yes." Walter nodded.

"He caused it." Aisha clenched her fingers around the treadmill handrail. "He turned you into..."

"He didn't cause anything," Walter said curtly. "At the end

of the day, I should have just gotten counseling. I should have talked about it. My MO is not to talk but to clam up and internalize everything. It worked against me in this case."

Aisha inhaled raggedly. "I can't see how you stand attending church with him as the pastor."

"At first I didn't want to, but now I have to keep an eye on him." Walter groaned, "I am the only one attending there who knows what he is capable of. He knows that I am watching him, he knows that he cannot afford a slip up with me around. If I leave, it will be fair game for some unsuspecting boy."

"And to think I complained about my day," Aisha muttered, "You have much more on your plate than I imagined."

"It is all better now, seeing you." Walter smiled. "You know you have always had that effect on me."

Aisha looked away from him and muttered under her breath. "You say the kind of things that make me want to love you."

"What was that?" Walter asked, slowing his pace on the treadmill.

"Nothing important." Aisha sighed.

****

Walter was sitting in his office on Friday when Cindy from HR, came up to his office with a bashful look on her face.

"Hey, Walter."

"Hey, Cindy." He was in the middle of a quarterly report for Guy's agro-business. He always gave a once over on all the reports under the Wiley Corp umbrella. Guy's manager, Winston had reported a glitch in the accounting system last quarter, and he was giving the report a thorough forensic once over. If one cent was missing, he would know. Cindy's appearance in his office was not very welcomed.

"Sorry to interrupt." Cindy read his body language correctly. "It's just that the first lady gave me her resume to work in the accounts department. We do have a vacancy, and she is well qualified. I thought I would come up here and plead her case..."

"No!" Walter shook his head before Cindy had even stopped speaking.

"But Walter, she is the first lady of our church." Cindy looked at him stubbornly, "I like her and did I mention she is well qualified."

"Yes, she is." Walter looked at the resume in Cindy's hand. "You can put that in the trash."

"Oh come on Walter," Cindy whined. "She is church family."

"That's right." Walter nodded, "and I try to hire as much qualified church family as I can but this a strong emphatic no."

Cindy glared at him. "You are mean."

"You don't know the meaning of mean." Walter fanned her out of his office.

Five minutes later he received a text from Gia.

It was worth a try.

He ignored it.

But that was the beginning of what he would mildly call Gia's assault. She saw him at Thursday's Homework session and waited for him in the parking lot.

"Walter, I am disappointed that you are still so unforgiving." Gia rested her hand on her hips and frowned at him grimly.

"I am not unforgiving." Walter shrugged, "I am just very wary of you."

Gia nodded. "I understand that I really do, but I am not the person I was then. I wish you would give me a chance to prove it."

Walter got into his vehicle and closed the door. "I don't know."

"Do you still find me attractive?" Gia asked softly, "Is that what this is about?"

Walter shook his head. "Gia, even if I found you attractive, you are a married woman and the first lady of this church. I am not even thinking about that. Besides, I remember what it was like to be burned by you. I am not interested."

Gia sighed. "That's fine. I am not ashamed to admit that I still think you are gorgeous and that I was stupid, way past stupid, for breaking up with you eight years ago. I was self-centered and foolish. I am mature enough to admit it."

Walter started the car. "Gia, please."

"Haven't you wondered what it would be like if I wasn't the kind of person I was then? You and I would still be together, and I would be happy."

Walter looked at her sharply. "You are unhappy now?"

Gia glanced at her watch. "I am fine Walter. Just dwelling in the what-if's."

Walter felt a pang of sympathy out of the blue, something that he didn't think he would ever feel toward Gia. Suddenly, he was curious about her and Axel. What was their home life like?

He shut down the feeling as quickly as it appeared and wished her a curt goodnight. She nodded.

"Goodnight Walter." Her voice sounded husky and choked up.

Walter looked back at her in the parking lot; she was standing waiting for Axel he assumed. She didn't have her own vehicle.

It took all his willpower not to offer her a lift home and not to question her about her present circumstance. He couldn't fall into Gia's net. He reminded himself of that all the way home.

Chapter Eighteen

Aisha had fallen into a routine with Walter. It was near the Easter holidays before she realized that she was in deeper trouble than she had first realized. It felt as if they spent all their spare time together.

She had taken up cooking. She wasn't particularly good at it, so Walter had offered to help. So they cooked together and hung out on his patio. They went to the gym together and swam most nights and had long lazy conversations about everything and nothing. It was all light and friendly and reminded her very much of their university days.

There was no repeat of the kiss between them and the heavy palpable tension that she felt in the earlier days had turned into a light, low humming tremor. She could see herself being Walter's friend, but just barely.

She had hot lurid dreams about him.

She wished she didn't, but she was a healthy normal female with a healthy libido and Walter could be the star of any woman's dream.

They went to a night cricket match at Sabina Park. Walter took his nephew, Pete with them.

Pete attended the school where she taught and was pretty popular with the teachers and extremely popular with the girls, which was not a surprise. He looked very much like his handsome father and uncles. Beyond his looks, he had a mature way about him and was unfailingly polite.

He called her Miss Fire and was quite excited to go with them to the match. They sat in the president's box by special invitation. It offered an unfettered view of the park. There were refreshments and a noisy crowd of society movers and shakers.

Pete grinned at her as she sat down in one of the plush chairs. "It's cool huh?"

"Yes." Aisha smiled. "Very cool."

A jovial senator, Theodore Pryce, hailed Walter and they engaged in a long conversation about his sisters.

Apparently, they were triplets; she got that much from eavesdropping. They were driving the senator crazy.

Pete leaned back in his chair. "Uncle Walter likes you. You should marry him."

Aisha glanced at Pete in surprise. "It's not that simple."

"It is." Pete nodded, "my dad says long courtships are frustrating for a man."

Aisha chuckled. "Really now?"

Pete grinned at her. "My mom said that they could play havoc on a woman too."

Aisha laughed. "I see."

"Uncle Walter doesn't have any girlfriends so you must be serious." Pete frowned, "You are his first girlfriend in years and years and years."

Aisha contemplated that and then answered cautiously.

"Maybe there is a reason for that."

"Yes, there is," Pete offered. "He doesn't play games with women's hearts. His words, not mine."

The game started and Walter joined them again. Aisha did not get the chance to set Pete straight. Obviously, he had no idea about his uncle, Walter.

There was a reason why Walter had not had a girlfriend in years, and it had nothing to do with playing with hearts. Pete was barking up the wrong tree. He was misguided in his thoughts about the uncle he obviously adored.

They had a good time at the match. The side that Aisha and Pete were rooting for won. Walter's side lost. Their first loss in thirteen matches.

Aisha and Pete, ribbed him all the way to the parking lot while he grumbled good-naturedly.

All bantering stopped however when they saw Axel Parks.

Aisha spotted him almost at the same time Walter did. He was with a young guy. They were laughing together, they got into his vehicle and drove off. Aisha couldn't remember where she had seen the boy before.

"Who is that with him?" She asked a tense Walter.

"Ivan Perkins. Elder Mary's grandson." Walter hissed.

Pete looked at his uncle quizzically. "You look angry uncle Walter."

"That's because I am," Walter muttered. "Angry and a little bit apprehensive."

"It could mean nothing." Aisha offered hopefully.

Walter shook his head. "The thing with Axel is, he bides his time, and then he becomes your confidant and friend."

Aisha sighed. "So what are you going to do about this?"

Walter looked at her. "I don't want to be the boy who cried wolf. "

"If the boy is in trouble, you should help," Pete said in the silence, "tell his parents. My dad said that I should tell him right away about weird stuff."

Walter looked at Pete. "Out of the mouth of babes."

"I am going to be fifteen soon." Pete snorted. "Hardly a babe."

Aisha grinned as Walter and Pete started bantering about his age. She listened to them, but deep down she was concerned.

And she was sure that Walter was as well. He was putting on a good front, but she could see his apprehension in the way his brow was furrowed. In the way, he gripped the steering wheel.

Aisha wondered if she should call Gia and alert her to what was happening. The very thought of reaching out to her cousin was abhorrent to her, and she ditched it as soon as it popped up. Gia wouldn't welcome her interference and would probably mock her about it somehow.

****

Walter attended church with a heaviness that he had not felt in a long time. He called Elder Mary as soon as he reached inside the house. He asked about Ivan and heard that he was home. He was very close to telling her about Axel and his past with him. He was so close.

And then she started singing Axel's praises.

"He is turning out to be a good influence on Ivan you know, Walter. Pastor White had Ivan getting B's in religious studies, but with this pastor, he is getting A's. Did you hear me, Walter, A's. My boy doesn't get A's."

"I hear you," Walter said, "I saw him tonight at the cricket match with Axel."

"Oh yes," Mary chuckled, "Pastor Axel loves his cricket,

doesn't he? He asked me to come along, but I declined. I am more of a tennis person myself. Did I tell you about my trip to Wimbledon? I went specifically to see Serena Williams win in 2008 or was it 2009? She is the greatest I tell you."

Mary rambled on and on, and Walter finally extricated himself from the conversation. He didn't tell her about Axel and his suspicions, and he spent most of the night tossing and turning about his decision to stay silent.

Maybe he was hyper-vigilant. Maybe he was reading too much into things, but he couldn't shake the thought that there were no warning signs when Axel made a move on him.

The next day he went to work feeling groggy and grumpy. At lunchtime, he went to the Yum Yum Cafe to order lunch and was in the middle of reading an engrossing article in the financial paper entitled: Food Is Where The Money Is. He liked the author's take on matters. Her research was impeccable.

"Hi, Walter."

Walter looked up. Gia was standing at the empty chair across from him, a tray in hand.

"May I join you?" She was dressed in a simple white outfit. Her make up was so understated he wasn't sure she had on any, and her hair was in a big curly bell that framed her face artfully. She looked angelic and sweet.

Walter blinked twice. He had never associated Gia with angels before, even when he was besotted with her.

"Er.. sure," He finally said.

"In the spirit of honesty, I must confess that I asked Cindy about you and she said you had lunch here most days." Gia smiled at him, and Walter had the feeling that she was launching a charm offensive.

He leaned back in his chair and drummed his fingers on the table. "Gia stalking me is not necessary, I am not going to hire you."

"I know, I know." Gia shrugged, "I just thought we could have lunch as friends."

Walter narrowed his eyes. "We were never friends. I don't think you know how to be a friend."

"I do," Gia said unperturbed. "I like to think I am Axel's closest friend."

"I saw him with Ivan last night at a cricket match," Walter said watching her closely. "He is not up to his old ways, is he Gia? Since you are his closest friend and he tells you his dark secrets, you would know wouldn't you?"

"I would." Gia nodded, "and there are no old ways. He made a mistake with you, only you, donkey years ago."

"I was seventeen." Walter snorted. "It was twelve years ago. Not exactly donkey years."

"He is a straight heterosexual male that got a little confused," Gia looked into her plate and then up at him, "I can assure you that we are a normal couple."

"Okay," Walter said doubtfully.

"Trust me. He is fine." Gia picked up her fork. "A perfect and attentive husband in and out of bed."

Walter narrowed his eyes. "If you say so."

"I say so." Gia grinned at him. "I knew you wanted to hear that. It was written all over your face."

"What I want to hear is that he is not secretly grooming Ivan." Walter leaned closer to her, "I have been toying with the idea of telling the elder's board about him."

"Oh Walter," Gia sighed and put down her fork. "Please don't. A reputation is such a hard thing to repair once it all goes through the gate. It can never be taken back. We are just humans. We do bad stuff sometimes. Stuff that we don't want to see the light of day. You have done things. Everyone on the elder's board has a skeleton or two or ten in their closet."

"So you are saying I should take Axel at face value and live and let live?"

"Exactly." Gia went back to her plate. "I would love the same courtesy extended to me too. I need a job, Walter. I love volunteering, but I cannot sit at home for a minute more. I want to drive my own car. I want to earn my own money."

Walter winced. It was jarring to hear her plead like this but hiring her was out of the question. He didn't want her in his space.

And then there was the little issue of her money laundering that she had told him about. She must have forgotten that. There was no way he would hire anyone with her record for his accounts department.

They did background checks on all their employees who handled money whether physically or electronically. He was just about to tell her that when he heard a familiar voice laughing in the cafeteria.

Gia looked up too and then smiled. "It's Greg Green!"

"This is like a reunion. The only person missing is Aisha, and then it would be like that date we went on that first time I met you."

"That's right," Gia smiled, "I forgot all about that."

It wasn't long before Greg spotted them and he greeted them loudly.

"Walter Wiley and Gia Fire! What a coincidence!"

"It's a small town," Walter murmured. He looked at Greg. He wasn't aging too well. He was developing a paunch, and his wavy hair was thinning at the top, and he had bags under his eyes. He looked ten years older.

Green drew up a chair without invitation and sat down. "Where should we start? We haven't seen each other in years!"

"I've seen you." Walter raised an eyebrow, "you showed that tape with me and Gia at a Chamber of Commerce party, forgot?"

"And I am sorry. You punished me for it, remember? My dad had to sell the company after you blacklisted us and I have to say it's the best thing you ever did. We love the bakery business. You even carry our products. I say let bygones be bygones. I have forgotten it and moved on."

Greg then turned to Gia, "but Miss Gia Fire, you are looking as gorgeous as the day you stepped on Mount Faith's campus. How is that possible?"

"God's blessings." Gia smiled at Greg. "I have been trying to convince Walter to let bygones be bygones and hire me."

"You don't say." Greg glanced at Walter. "He is not very forgiving you know. "

"I am forgiving enough to allow you to sell your stuff at all our locations." Walter snorted. "If I still had a grudge against you, that would not happen."

"Well," Greg looked at Walter contemplatively, "I take it back, you are forgiving and thank you. You are a better man than I am."

Gia tucked her hand under her chin and looked at Greg. "That tape had me on it too. I have no idea if I should be mad at you."

"Don't be. I er short-circuited for a little bit." Greg cleared his throat. "The perils of jealousy I guess. I thought Walter was having a better life than I was and I had a little competition with him going on in my head. It was uncalled for and terribly wrong. I apologized to him and destroyed the tape, and now I am apologizing to you as well."

"Apology accepted," Gia said readily. "See how easy that was Walter?"

"He tried to ruin my reputation in the business community."

alter snorted, "a good reputation is hard to win and easy to lose. It is because of what Greg did to me, why I pause before making a move with Axel."

Gia nodded. "I see."

"I accepted Greg's apology, and he got his punishment." Walter paused, "Axel was never punished for what he did to me."

Greg looked between him and Gia. "Who is Axel? And what did he do to you?"

"Her husband and what he did to me is not information for public consumption," Walter said. "You understand don't you?"

Greg held up his hand. "I do. I mind my own business."

Gia cleared her throat loudly. "Er Greg...You wouldn't happen to have a position available at the bakery, would you? I am job hunting."

"As a matter of fact there are several vacancies in admin, we just expanded our head office."

Gia reached for her bag, "I have a resume."

Greg took it and looked at her ring finger pointedly.

Walter watched the tableaux in front of him without much emotion. He didn't think a Greg/Gia alliance was a good idea. He could almost predict how this was going to go down.

Greg would hire Gia, not because of her qualifications, but because she was the one that got away. He had been pretty smitten with her in university. He had been torn up when Gia had dumped him like a sack of potatoes.

And now the tables were turned, he had the upper hand. He would be drunk with the power of being her boss.

He would instigate an affair. Gia would probably give in and ensnare him thus gaining the upper hand again. And the game would go on.

Unless, of course, she had really changed and was a true

christian. Somehow he doubted that. It wasn't a far stretch imagining Gia using seduction to her advantage. She had deliberately sought him out today dressed to appear innocent yet seductive.

And now she was looking at Greg and giving him a slow, sultry smile that was guaranteed to get the fickle Greg drawn in her net or at least get her the job.

Greg scanned through the resume and smiled. "I need an admin assistant, but you seem to be overqualified for it."

"I'll take it," Gia said quickly. "I will take anything."

Greg smiled slowly. "Well, okay then. Report for work tomorrow. Here's my number I'll give you directions to the office."

"Gia is married to my church pastor." Walter felt obliged to point out.

"Is that so?" Greg broke eye contact with Gia and looked at Walter. "I don't mind."

Translation: he wasn't particular about seeing a married woman.

Walter looked at Gia. "You don't have to do this. You know what the outcome of this will be."

"I have no idea what you are talking about Walter," Gia dismissed his concerns easily.

Walter shook his head. "Well, let me leave you two new coworkers to it."

He could feel Gia's stare as he left the cafe.

Chapter Nineteen

Aisha was leaving work when her mother called to chat. Her mother usually had her hand on the pulse of the Fire family. And she ran through the various woes and triumphs of her brothers and sisters and nieces and nephews without much participation from Aisha.

"And Gia got a job," Grace said, "She is working at a bakery, well the admin office. She is excited about it."

"Good for her," Aisha murmured.

"I gave her your address," Grace said helpfully, "she wanted to visit."

"Mom, no." Aisha groaned. "Why? Why? Why?"

"She is your cousin, and she wants to reach out," Grace said stubbornly, "you need to meet her halfway."

"I do not want to reach out to her," Aisha got into her car with a huff. "I am fine with our relationship as it is."

"But she is family!" Grace exclaimed, "what's the matter with you, Aisha?"

"I can't argue with you mom," Aisha said tiredly, "but please do not give my address to anyone else without my permission."

"Okay," Grace said chastised.

Aisha hung up the phone feeling a little put out with her mother. Now Gia had access to where she lived, a part of her still didn't trust her cousin. Too many years of being burned will do that to a person.

She drove toward home but stopped at her favorite clothing store. The clothes were expensive, but she usually budgeted to get one outfit a month. This time she was getting herself a new swimsuit and some work out clothes.

She liked de-stressing with exercise especially because she got to hang with Walter. And as usual thinking about Walter brought a goofy grin on her face. It was totally uncalled for, but she just couldn't help it.

She was rifling through the bikinis when a pink one caught her eye. And then she glanced above the mirrors and saw Axel Parks. Gia's husband.

The Queen G herself was right behind him in a green halter-top dress and a face full of makeup. She looked like a doll.

They headed toward her, but they hadn't seen her yet.

Aisha ducked behind a clothing rack and turned her back, hoping against hope that she wouldn't be spotted.

She could hear them though, and she could see Axel clearly. Luckily, he was focused on the rack of clothes in front of him.

"I don't understand why you are so eager to work," Axel said clearly, "you would be better off at home, living a quiet life.

"Like a retired person?" Gia huffed. "I am twenty-eight years old not eighty-two. I need to engage my mind."

"Then volunteer at church." Axel pulled out a dress and then showed it to Gia. "This is not bad."

"It looks like something a shapeless person would wear." Gia grunted, "look at this one."

Aisha couldn't see what she was holding up, but Axel was shaking his head in disbelief. "No, you are a first lady, not a promiscuous loose woman."

"This would not make me look promiscuous. It's an ordinary decent looking piece of material." Gia hissed. "Sometimes you act so pious I feel like reminding you where you are coming from."

"I knew we shouldn't have come back to Jamaica," Axel murmured, "It is tearing us apart."

"Well, we couldn't have stayed in Florida. Gia rejoined, "because you had to go and revisit your old habits and get caught by my father of all people. Don't blame this move on me!"

Aisha didn't wait to hear Axel's response. She made a mad dash to the door. She dearly hoped that they wouldn't see her, but they were too busy sparring to really notice anyone.

****

Walter left his meeting with the vice presidents at approximately eight o'clock. He had several missed calls, and he rifled through his phone. Most of them were from Gia. The latest one was just two minutes before.

He called her back on his way to the parking lot.

"Walter, thank God." Gia breathed in his ear. "I've been calling everybody I can. Can you pick me up, please? I am stranded."

"Where?" Walter asked getting into his car.

"At church. I do Tuesday classes. Axel was supposed to

pick me up, and he is not answering his phone. The janitor is keeping me company all the persons with vehicles have already left."

Walter considered saying no. And then reluctantly said yes. What kind of person would he be if he ignored a person in genuine distress? Even if the person was Gia.

He turned on a radio program to keep him company while he drove on the way to the church.

When he pulled up into the churchyard, she was sitting on the porch with Charlie, the janitor. He lived on the church grounds in a small cottage.

Walter waved to Charlie when he drove up, and Gia got into the car.

"Thank you so much, Walter," Gia said breathlessly. "I knew you would come when I called. You've always been a genuine and kind person."

Walter glanced at Gia's distressed face and nodded.

"You are welcome. Are you staying at the church house on Waterloo Road?"

"Yes." Gia nodded. She settled in the seat. "Thanks again, Walter."

Walter shrugged. "No problem."

"I need a vehicle," Gia muttered. "I seriously need a vehicle. I am desperate enough to take up Greg's offer to use his spare car for the interim."

Walter drove out of the churchyard before he spoke. "So where is Axel?"

"I have no clue." Gia sighed. "I went to the interview with Greg today, and I got the job."

"Naturally," Walter murmured.

Gia looked at him crossly. "I am more than qualified for that job."

"I didn't say anything." Walter looked at her, "you are

setting up yourself for an affair. You know that."

"No, I am not." Gia huffed, "I never really liked Greg. He's too..."

"Eager." Walter finished for her, "and now he is offering you his spare car."

Gia glared at him mutinously. "You need to take your mind out of the gutter."

"Okay." Walter turned up the program on the radio and ignored Gia.

Gia turned the volume down looked at Walter. "Do you want the truth?"

"About what?" Walter glanced at her curiously.

Gia licked her lips and then looked away from him. "The truth about me and Axel and me and you at university..."

Walter nodded. "Sure."

"I loved you too back then. Remember when you told me and I was very mean to you."

"Yes, will never forget it." Walter inhaled. "You created quite a scene."

"I don't know what came over me," Gia shrugged, "panic I guess. I regretted it ever since. And then after the issue with the tape at university and my dad's disapproval, I felt so depressed; I truly didn't care what I did with myself in my early twenties."

Walter cleared his throat. "Okay."

"And so I told you about my drug habit and Axel finding me," Gia bit her lip, "I was very grateful to him for sticking by me through my dark times. I was riddled with guilt, trust me. I told him everything about my life, and he still stayed and then he told me everything about him and I accepted him as is. I guess I felt as if we were kind of kindred spirits, you know. We had a bond of sorts."

Walter glanced at her. "Bond over badness."

"Something like that." Gia sighed. "We knew each other's dark sides, and we still were fine with each other. So he proposed a year after and I accepted, not because I loved him. I found that I couldn't love anyone after you. My first and last love."

Gia inhaled raggedly, "and then I came here and you are here. I must admit old feelings are coming back. We were good together weren't we Walter?"

"No, we weren't. I don't have fond memories of that time with you. The break-up kind of took care of that."

"I could make up for it," Gia said earnestly, "I could..."

"No." Walter almost barked it. "Stop it Gia. Right now. Pack up that thought and shove it to the back, the very back of your mind. I am not interested."

Gia sighed loudly. "I am so unhappy."

"Talk that over with the man you married." Walter was glad to see the road where the house was on.

"I don't have my spare keys," Gia said helplessly. "I am going to have to wait for Axel to get home."

Walter stopped at the gate and looked over at the house in darkness. It was a relatively safe street. They had twenty-four-hour security thankfully because he was seriously contemplating kicking Gia out of the car.

He did not want to be reminiscing with her. He didn't want to feel sorry for her. He didn't want to hear about her past love for him. He didn't want to soften his stance on Gia. It would be too easy to fall under her spell.

He would be lying if he didn't acknowledge that Gia being vulnerable and regretful about their past was giving him a certain buzz. What was that feeling— triumph, vindication?

She turned tearful eyes to him and then sniffed. "When I make love to Axel, I think about you, Walter."

She ran a hand up his leg, slowly.

Walter closed his eyes and then opened them. He grasped her hand in his and said gruffly.

"Gia, get out of the car!"

Gia looked at him pleadingly. "Say the word Walter, and I'll leave Axel tonight. Now."

Walter reached past her, pulled the seat belt and then opened the door. "Out. Get out!"

Gia took one look at his mutinous expression and scrambled out of the car.

Walter closed the door behind her and drove off without a backward glance.

His phone rang when he was near his home. He didn't answer. He didn't want to have to deal with Gia again. He let it ring out. When it started ringing again, he saw that it was Mary calling.

He answered her a little snappier than he wanted to, it was a delayed reaction to Gia and her seduction routine.

But Mary didn't seem to realize. She sounded worried.

"Walter, have you seen Ivan? He is not back from the homework program at church."

"No," Walter said absently. "Thursdays are my days, not Tuesdays. Have you called his phone?"

"Yes!" Mary said in heightened panic. "Harding was supposed to drop him home. Harding said he never showed up at the classes tonight."

Walter felt suddenly nauseous what were the odds? Ivan was missing. Axel was missing. He was jumping to all sorts of conclusions.

"I am going to call his parents," Mary said and hung up.

Walter drove home his hands shaking. If anything happened to Ivan, it would be his fault. He should have told the elders what he knew about Axel. He sat in the driveway unable to move, believing the worst.

Chapter Twenty

Aisha sat at the edge of the pool and flicked the water with her toes lazily. She had done six laps and was feeling fatigued. The conversation from earlier was churning in her head. Axel had gone back to his old habits and gotten caught?

What old habits was Gia talking about? Aisha worried her bottom lip with her teeth. She was waiting for Walter, but his car was not in the driveway nor was there any light in his house. She had come to the gym to try to make sense of the conversation.

She was itching to tell Walter. Maybe his suspicions as it related to Axel were not so far off after all. She did one more lap sluicing through the water at a leisurely pace. What were Axel Park's old habits?

She floated on her back and then her belly and then decided to call it a night. She was exhausted. It must be close to nine o'clock, and she couldn't wait up for Walter she was feeling wiped.

She was surprised to see Walter parked in his driveway and sitting in his car. He wasn't on his phone. He was just sitting there.

She walked up to the car and knocked on the glass twice before Walter reacted. He jumped a little and then wound down the window.

"Hey, Aisha." His voice was tired. He looked slightly ruffled.

"What's going on?" Aisha asked. "You look like you have seen a ghost."

"Axel is missing, won't answer his phone and the same with Ivan."

"Uh oh," Aisha widened her eyes. "Are you thinking that he..."

"Yes!" Walter ran his hand over his face. "I am thinking exactly that."

"Today I overheard Gia and Axel in a clothing store," Aisha whispered, "Gia accused him of going back to his old habits and being caught by the Bishop. Do you think that's the old habit she was referring to?"

Walter groaned and rested his head on the steering wheel. "I don't know, if it is I am not without fault. I should have said something. I saw Axel and Ivan at the cricket match and I still didn't act. I knew having Gia and Axel back in my life would screw things up."

"What are you going to do?" Aisha asked.

"Wait," Walter murmured. "There is nothing else to do. I just dropped Gia home because Axel isn't answering his phone. I have no idea where to look. Mary is searching around for Ivan. So I just have to wait."

A wave of sleepiness washed over Aisha, and she blinked her eyes rapidly and then opened them.

"You look tired," Walter said softly.

"I am, was waiting for you by the pool. Did too many laps."

"Go to bed. I'll bring you up to date tomorrow." Walter smiled at her.

Her belly did a double flip. As usual, seeing Walter's smile did something to her inside.

Walter was a devastatingly attractive man. And he had an effect on her that was unprecedented.

"Goodnight." She kept her friendly voice on. It was becoming harder and harder to be Walter's friend. She was going to start looking for an apartment first thing tomorrow.

"Goodnight Aisha," Walter said softly.

She left him still sitting in his vehicle, and she slowly walked to her front door. She would miss this place, but she had to go. It was time she started withdrawing from Walter's orbit.

****

One hour later Walter was sitting on the patio with his phone in hand. He called Mary for the umpteenth time, and she finally answered.

"Yes, Walter, he is home," Mary said sheepishly, "I forgot that he had an appointment at the orthodontist. His Dad had put his phone on silent."

Walter breathed a sigh of relief. "Okay, good to hear."

Mary hung up, and Walter contemplated calling her back and telling her why he was anxious about Axel and Ivan. He had spent too many hours stressing over Axel and where he could be and who he could be grooming. It was becoming tiring. He couldn't live his life like this.

He picked up the phone and was on the verge of calling and then changed his mind.

He went into the house, rifled through his library and found one of the church programs with Axel's number on it.

He dialed it instead. He didn't know what he was going to say he just knew that something had to be said.

He didn't expect Axel to answer the phone, Gia had said he was hard to reach, but he did answer.

"Axel," Walter said without preamble. "I trust you are home now?"

"Yes," Axel said cautiously, "Gia told me you dropped her home. Thank you. My phone battery died on me while I was at the hospital with the Linton's to give them some support. Did you know their little girl Sadie was hit by a car?"

"No." Walter inhaled, "How is she?"

"Broken ribs, broken leg." Axel sighed, "but thank the lord she will be okay."

"Have you really changed Axel?" Walter got to the point, "because let me tell you, I am at a complete loss as to what to do about you. One thing is for sure I cannot continue to spend my days worried that one day you will try to do something with some young man at my church."

Axel sighed down the phone. "Walter, I am not planning to do any harm to anyone. I wasn't even planning to rape you when your brothers caught me. I wasn't naked because I was about to jump you or anything. Nor was I undressing you to rape you. I had this desire to er..."

"To what?" Walter growled.

"To be a girl, okay. I wanted to pretend that I was a girl. I was going to dress up in some female clothes and pretend you were my date. It was a fantasy. I certainly never thought of rape."

Walter didn't know what to say. He sat on a bar stool hard. "So what are you saying? You are just a benign transvestite who drugged me so that you could play dress up and pretend? I am as confused as ever because I can vividly remember before I passed out that you kissed me."

"I was curious about how it would feel so I kissed you." Axel sighed. "But I swear I am not interested in men. I went through a confused stage. I toyed with the idea for a while. I even thought I was in love with your brother, Jordan but it passed. And before you say it, no I am not in denial about my sexuality, I know this for sure."

"I don't know if I can trust you, Axel," Walter said, "I am this close to outing you to the elder's board. I cannot be your secret keeper. It's not fair to me. I was a victim of whatever twisted sickness you have."

"Wait! No!" Axel sounded as if he was hyperventilating, "Walter I swear I am not a predator or a pervert. I could swear on a stack of Bibles if you wanted me to."

"No thanks. Pastor's swearing on Bibles mean nothing to me." Walter snapped. "Tell me one thing, why are you back in Jamaica?"

"Because I," Axel groaned. "Bishop Fire caught me in female clothes at a local restaurant. I didn't know he would recognize me. I sometimes like to dress up and go out. I put on makeup, some nice things and I hit the streets."

Walter gasped. "Say what now?"

"The Bishop couldn't deal with it, said I had a touch of the devil and asked me to leave his church. Who can blame him, I was married to his daughter and he found me in one of her dresses."

Walter laughed out loud. "Axel you are nuttier than a box of nuts."

"I am struggling with cross-dressing and being in touch with my feminine side. I am not nutty." Axel said defensively. "I am praying about it. I want victory over it. That is my current trial, not young boys."

"Lord give me strength," Walter whispered. "So this cross-dressing madness, does Gia know about it?"

"She does." Axel sighed. "I genuinely love Gia. I can't believe she is in my life. I mean, I can't believe a man like me got so lucky."

"You two, need counseling," Walter said sternly.

"Does this mean, you won't out me?" Axel asked anxiously.

"It means I'll think about it," Walter mused. "If you don't get counseling I am outing you. And another thing, Gia came on to me tonight. Keep her out of my way. If she even attempts to say anything to me that is not above par, I am outing the two of you."

Axel paused. "Yes, I understand."

"Two for one package Axel." Walter warned. "If you slip even once, I am telling the whole church not only the elder's board about you and your wife."

"I hear you," Axel said relief in his voice.

"And stay away from Ivan," Walter said, "no excuses."

"Yes, I will," Axel muttered, "he is a bright young man, he just learns differently from us."

"Then tell his grandmother and let her get him professional help." Walter snapped. "No more alone time with Ivan or else I am going to out you. Be on your best behavior, Axel."

He hung up the phone and sighed in relief. He could rest easy tonight.

****

The beginning of summer came with a bang and the kind of heat that was expected from Kingston.

Walter was feeling a bit more comfortable at church. He could stomach Axel's presence in his life a little easier since their talk. He sat through his sermons when he preached and didn't feel like gagging.

Gia was avoiding him too, no more confessions about

love. She finally got her own vehicle, a black Mini Cooper; hence no more distress calls from her in the night.

His life was almost back to normal. He still kept a wary eye on Axel, but he had stuck to his end of the bargain as far as Walter could see and was keeping his distance from Ivan and the rest of the young men at church.

The only fly in his ointment these days was Aisha Fire. She had told him solemnly that she was planning to leave. Her house hunting irked him. He resented the fact that she wanted to leave.

They spent loads of time together especially on weekends and went to Guy's farm several times because Aisha had fallen in love with the place.

He had kept his distance since the kiss and kept their relationship on a friendly undemanding level, but he found that he wanted more. Much more. Maybe he should announce to her that he was in courtship mode so that there was no mistaking what he was about.

He didn't want to crowd her, but it was time they both addressed the attraction between them. According to Shawn, the air sizzled when they were together. He was inclined to believe his sister-in-law.

He left work early and impulsively got her flowers; a dozen long-stemmed red roses with the thorns removed.

When he got home, he saw that her car was in the driveway. He knocked on the door, left the roses and disappeared into his house. He was going to up the charm offensive whether she liked it or not. Things were about to get really serious.

****

April

He started sending her lines from songs. He wasn't into

writing poems, so verses from songs would have to do.

He was sure that the one from Boris Gardener, I Wanna Wake Up With You was more than obvious enough. What could be more blatant than, *I wanna wake up with you, I wanna be there when you open your eyes...?*

He continued the charm offensive with chocolate. She liked Ferrero Rocher. He got cases of it from the supplier who delivered it to the supermarket. He made a special order and had it delivered to his office.

Preston saw the delivery guy and then came to his office and looked around. "What's all this? A wedding? A party?"

"No, a courtship," Walter grumbled. "The girl says she wants to be courted in an old-fashioned way and this is her favorite chocolate. I am going to give it to her one gift at a time."

Preston chuckled. "I have never seen you try so hard with a woman."

"That's true. She's the first because she is special. I can't forget that she found it quite easy to ignore me in university." Walter growled. "So I turned up the charm, but she is not responding."

"Maybe you shouldn't be so subtle," Preston said, "just tell her outright that you like her."

"Love her," Walter corrected.

Preston grinned. "Just tell her."

"Or maybe she wants me to court her some more." Walter mused. "I have been the proper gentleman so far."

Preston shook his head. "You'll give her diabetes if you take it too slow."

May

Guy stopped by his office with a basket full of strawberries.

"Strawberry season bro," Guy said, "April to July on my farm is the most wonderful time of the year."

"I know," Walter mused, "I'll give these to Aisha." He sniffed the fragrant basket.

"She loves them, doesn't she?" Guy said proudly.

"Yes. She makes a little squeal when I deliver them to her and claps her hands and then hugs me tight. Her body fits perfectly to mine. You know she is slim, but she has the perfect curves. And we do exercise together a lot. Me, to cut down on the sexual energy. She, well I don't know why she works out as hard as I do."

"For the same reason." Guy shook his head. "You two need to talk. It should go like this, 'Aisha I love you, I want to bang you. Let's get married before I do something stupid.' And she'll say, 'I thought you'd never ask, Walter.' And then you'll live happily ever after."

Walter shook his head. "I don't think so. She doesn't find me irresistible, yet. You'll have to keep the strawberries coming."

"Well, when you find out why she is ignoring you and you finally propose," Guy said cheekily. "The wedding trellis is blooming. It is going to be spectacular in my east garden. Perfect wedding spot."

June

Jordan and Shawn were in his office working out a multi-million dollar budget for a project that would be financed by Wiley Corp and developed by them, when he had flowers delivered to the office so that he could take it home to Aisha.

The florists were making a pretty penny off him. He ordered small bouquets for her every Tuesday but today was her birthday and the first day of her summer holiday, so it was special, and it was huge.

"For Aisha?" Jordan raised an eyebrow.

"Her birthday," Walter said pointing to the balloon, which read *happy birthday*.

"You've been trying for months and not getting anywhere with her," Shawn said, "We've all been watching and discussing your situation."

"You nosy Wiley's need to mind your own business," Walter growled. "I've got this."

"No, you don't." Shawn snorted. "The problem we have is that we like to see you happy. So this is what I am going to do."

Shawn grabbed the phone. "I am going to have a chat with Aisha and tell her to stop being a stubborn mule about you."

"Shawn, seriously, put down the phone." Walter leaned forward in his chair. "Leave it alone. Talk to her Jordan."

Jordan shook his head. "I agree with her. Walter, women are always beating down your door for you to pay them some attention. If you were giving just a smidgen to any of these women, I don't know what they would do.

"Remember that supermarket cashier we had to fire because she was stalking you? Or that lady at church who was going to commit suicide if you didn't love her back?"

"Yes, so what?" Walter barked, "What matters here is that the woman I love doesn't want anything to do with me, even though I am doing exactly what she wants me to do with this whole courtship thing."

"Something is wrong with Aisha!" Shawn said indignantly, "She is getting the full hundred watt attention from a gorgeous, successful, god fearing, sexy..."

"Hold on a minute," Jordan turned to Shawn, "you sound too much into this description."

Shawn laughed. "Look at him, Jordan, your brother, is

gorgeous. Look at those biceps."

Walter flexed his biceps dutifully.

Shawn pretended to swoon.

Jordan chuckled. "Okay, carry on."

"This girl is either blind, deaf, dumb or a lesbian." Shawn shook her head.

"She is none of those things," Walter protested. "And what's more, I told her about my past. I told her everything. The thing with Axel, and Gia and the tape, the truth is she seemed okay with all of it, and this was months ago..."

"The question is," Shawn leaned forward in her chair dramatically, "does she think you are blind, deaf, dumb or gay?"

"She wouldn't think..." Walter halted, and then he struggled to remember a puzzling conversation that they had about secrets with Aisha. It made total sense now. He was dropping her to work, and she had asked him about his church being liberal, and then there was a moment of telling silence, and then she had said that Gia had told her his secret.

What was the secret that Gia had told Aisha? He needed to hear what it was? *Was it something that had grossed her out badly?*

He had told Aisha everything already but what had Gia said to her? Had she gone into details about some of their steamier times?

"I think I just discovered something," Walter murmured, "I need to call Gia to solve this mystery."

Chapter Twenty-One

It was sheer laziness that had Aisha skipping through the classifieds and finding fault with all the rental listings. It was a good time to house hunt. School was out, so she had three months of holiday, and time to check out all options at her leisure.

The truth was, she didn't want to move. She had several reasons. The location was relatively close to her school. It was free accommodation, her landlord if you could call Guy that, was grateful for her to house sit because he hardly came by and the biggest reason of all—she loved living beside Walter.

She munched through a box of Ferrero Rocher that Walter had left on her doorstep and skipped through the newspaper lazily. Walter was leaving her chocolate and flowers and music and fixing dinners. He was the perfect boyfriend, and she had no idea why?

If she didn't know better, she would call him romantic. If

she didn't know better, she would think he was courting her. If she didn't know better, she would think that their outings and their private dinners with just the two of them on his back patio were more than just hanging as friends.

But she knew better.

So far they were closer than ever. They talked about everything from her wanting to have kids as soon as possible to what she was looking for in a man.

She never asked him any questions about that. She skirted the issue. She didn't want to hear Walter describing what he wanted in a man. It would make her feel icky. She wasn't in any way homophobic; it's just that she couldn't stand the thought of Walter being with a man. Not her Walter.

She was living in a perfect bubble right now, and she did not want Walter to burst it to remind her that her perfect world was not so perfect.

This was the beginning of summer, and they had several things planned. They were going to visit his side of Portland; they were going to go rafting on the Blue Lagoon and...

Her phone buzzed, and she looked at it eagerly thinking it was Walter. Maybe he was inviting her to lunch. She had never been to the Yum Yum Cafe, though she had food from there when Walter brought it home.

It was a text from Gia. She hadn't heard from Gia in weeks. *Coming over later, happy birthday by the way.*

Aisha groaned.

She racked her brain for some response that would not be too ungracious. She didn't want to see Gia.

She texted back: *I might not be here.*

She didn't get a response. She waited for the rest of the day but got nothing.

When her phone rang in the evening, and she saw that it was Gia, Aisha ignored it.

Let Gia think that she wasn't there. She didn't expect that five minutes later she would hear a knock on the door. She groaned out loud. Someone had let her in. The Wiley Brothers were slacking up on their security for the complex.

She yanked the door open and put on her most unwelcoming face.

It was Gia... and Walter.

"You let her in!" Aisha accused.

"I did." Walter nodded. "She has something to say to you. I need you to hear it. This won't take long. "

Gia wasn't looking particularly pleased to be there.

"I er..." Gia cleared her throat. "I lied to you about Walter being gay. He and I had a year-long relationship, and we broke up.

"Then I saw you two together around campus, and I got jealous, so I lied to you then. I had to make up something to break you two apart because I realized what a fool I had been and I wanted him back for myself. The thing is, I am too proud to beg so I stayed away, but I had no intentions of you getting him, so I told you something to devastate you."

Aisha swallowed audibly. "What?"

"And then when I came back to Jamaica, and I saw Walter again, I realized afresh how stupid I was to have given him up and I saw that you two were getting close so I lied to you again."

"You have never liked seeing me happy, Gia." Aisha growled, "since I was a little girl."

"That's true." Gia blinked back tears, "I don't know if you can forgive me, Aisha."

She then turned her puppy dog fake teary eyes to Walter and touched him on the arm. "I am so sorry, Walter..."

"Take your hands off my man witch," Aisha said fiercely, "thank you for finally telling me the truth but I don't know if

I can ever trust you again."

"I'll escort her out," Walter said a satisfied smile on his face.

What was he smiling about? Aisha thought pitifully. She had just heard that she had wasted too many years of her life thinking that he was gay.

And the last couple of months had been a study in frustration. Walter had been courting her, and she hadn't even recognized it!

She had thought Walter was just being Walter.

She did a quick twirl in the hall mirror; she was in one of her favorite casual dresses, bright yellow with white flowers. Her hair was in fluffy curls around her shoulders, and her eyes were bright and happy. Her excitement was suddenly at fever pitch. Walter Wiley had been courting her!

Proper old-fashioned courtship, just as she had requested and she hadn't even realized it.

"Hey," Walter knocked on the door with a large gift basket in his hand. "Happy Birthday."

"Thank you," Aisha took the basket from him set it on the entrance table and hugged him. "Today is the happiest day of my life."

Walter chuckled in her hair. "And why is that?"

"I can see clearly now, the lies are gone, and I am free from agonizing about you. I can say it loud and firmly; I love you, Walter Wiley. For ages and ages and you wouldn't believe how happy I am that I can finally say it out loud."

"I believe you because I love you too." Warm fingers cupped her cheekbone as he bent his dark head. He captured her moist lips in a devouring kiss.

He pulled away before they could get any more heated.

"Would you like a big engagement production or a simple, heartfelt one?" Walter asked.

Aisha looked into his eyes. "I hate productions. I prefer heartfelt and private. That's why I have to ask, Walter will you marry me?"

Walter laughed. "Of course I will. You stole my line, and since I have been doing this the old-fashioned way, I'll have to ask your mother and stepfather for your fair hand first.

He pulled her closer.

"But privately I have to say, I pledge to you my heart, and I intend to make you my wife very soon."

****

They got married on Guy's farm under the strawberry trellis which was in full fragrant fruit. It was the perfect day—cool and sunny with just the right amount of breeze.

The bride wore a simple off the shoulder white dress, and the groom was in a tux that emphasized his very toned physique.

Pastor Tate officiated.

Most of Aisha's family was there with one glaring exception, Gia and her husband, Axel.

They had a farm style reception with strawberry bowls as centerpieces. The backdrop to the reception area was breathtaking enough for them not to need many decorations.

The brothers gathered near the back of the tent and watched as Walter and his bride had their first dance.

"They look perfect together," Jordan said a proud tilt to his head.

Preston clicked his glass to Jordan's. "I am just happy he married the right Fire girl."

"May their lives be happy and blessed," Saint said, "you will not believe the wedding present I have for Walter."

Guy looked at him sharply. "What are you planning?"

"Axel is the reason, I even entered the security field," Saint said solemnly, "he hurt my brother, and I vowed that he wouldn't get away with it. I am not planning anything. I am just going to keep a close eye on him. He'd better be perfect after this because Saint Wiley is back in town."

"I almost feel sorry for the bugger." Preston grinned. "Here's to Walter's happiness."

Epilogue

Elder's meeting a month later after his honeymoon was almost as solemn as it was at the beginning of the year. He had not been plugged in. He had spent the last two weeks off the grid.

Walter walked into the meeting later than everybody else.

Everyone was dour-faced and somber.

"Who died?" Walter asked, sitting at his usual spot around the boardroom table.

"Nobody." Elder Harding passed his tablet down the table toward Walter. It was opened to an article entitled: *Pastor and Wife Exposed.*

There was no commentary. Just pictures with captions. The first picture was of Axel in a tight red dress with a curly wig and makeup. It was captioned: *Pastor Axel Parks Of The Pine Grove Church Having A Night Out On The Town.*

Beneath that was a picture of Gia with no clothes in a lewd position smiling at the camera sultrily. Her privates were pixelated but still shocking enough to make him gasp. It was captioned: *First Lady Gia In Her Lover's Bed.*

The third picture was of Axel whispering in some man's ear. The person captioned it, *Sweet Nothings.*

The fourth was of Gia passionately kissing Greg in what looked like a parking lot. It was captioned: *The Boss And The First Lady.*

Walter frowned grimly. He had told Axel to seek help.

"So where are they now?" He asked aloud.

"The pastor is fired. And he may face criminal charges for having a questionable relationship with a minor in Florida, apparently the same person who went after him, also has more evidence," Elder Mary said grimly. "As for the first lady she is shacking up with her lover, Greg Green, her boss."

"You could have told us Elder Walter. You could have saved us this embarrassment. This does not look good on our church."

"I am not a fortune teller. I couldn't predict that these two would fall so spectacularly from grace," Walter said, "What I knew about Axel and Gia was from their past, they said they had changed. This is the present. This cannot be on me."

"You could have given us a heads up!" Elder Mary gritted. "I begged you to tell me."

"And that would have been wrong. It would have smeared them before they could prove themselves," Walter said. "I battled myself with this. I wanted to say something, but you see, time has a way of showing the genuine from the counterfeit. I firmly believe people can change, because I did and so I was willing to give them both the benefit of the doubt. As it is they proved me wrong."

Mary opened her mouth and then closed it again.

"Well, I'll be," Elder Donald, muttered, "Mary has nothing to say to that."

Elder Harding said in the silence. "Welcome back Elder Walter and congratulations on the marriage. May God be in your union. Put him first."

"Thank you and I will," Walter nodded, only half listening when they moved on to other business.

He surreptitiously checked his phone; it was blinking with two messages.

I told you I wouldn't rest until Axel Parks was brought to justice, no ministry will take that man now. You can thank me later, Saint

Walter shook his head, so he was the one who had released the photographs.

He then checked his other message from Aisha. *Love you, babe.*

Love you more, he texted back.

The End

"Stop talking to Guy Wiley. Stop entertaining him. Stop mooning over him. He is good looking yes, nobody can deny that, but he is as poor as a church mouse."

Lucia glared at her mother. She was not mooning over Guy Wiley. So she had been caught looking at a picture that she had taken of him when he was in his uncle Micky's field.

He had been shirtless. He posed with his hand on a hoe, surrounded by a barren, just plowed field. He looked out in the distance at the lush greenery that was the Rio Grande Valley. It was a beautiful photo. It showed the raw beauty of the valleys and its subject was a man who did not look like the stereotypical farmer. He hadn't even known she took the picture. Guy was not for posing and that kind of model stuff.

Her mother could not see the loveliness of the composition or the vividness of the colors. Her mother saw things in black and white—money or no money, rich or poor, farmer or doctor.

For her mother, taking pictures was a pointless hobby, and talking to Guy Wiley, the only person in her life that seemed to understand her was meaningless. They had been too poor for too long for her to be flirting with the idea of spending her time taking pretty pictures or talking to pretty boys.

Her mother wanted her to marry the doctor. She said it more than ten times a day and double that on the weekends. And she was about to lecture her about it now.

Lucia looked at her and put away the pictures. She figured that now would not be a good time to tell her mom that she had gotten a wedding gig, a paying gig. The wedding was that of a relative of a coworker from the supermarket.

Chad had seen some of her pictures, showed it to his sister and now she was hired. The only problem was that the wedding was in Kingston and she needed some more equipment to really wow her clients.

Her savings account had in just enough funds so the bank wouldn't close it and her next four paychecks were already spent, the roof of their three-bedroom cottage needed fixing.

The roof was a sieve. Every time it rained they had to find additional buckets to catch water at strategic locations throughout the house. It had drizzled today, and there was a staccato drip, drip sound that could be heard like an off-key choir.

It could be worse, Lucia supposed. A few years ago before they moved to the valleys, they had no floor or even roof. They had thrown a tarpaulin over the bare concrete walls when it rained and that had been their shelter.

Those were lean years. Lucia and her brothers barely survived it. They had even lived at the poorhouse once; it had been a better experience than where they were in Norwich. Her mother's husband, Nate's father, had almost killed them in a house fire there.

And then someone had mentioned to her mother that her distant relative had died leaving a house in the valleys. Her mother had packed them up and moved to the valleys anticipating a house of their own only to find a one-room shed.

They were still grateful; living in a poorhouse had negative connotations that was hard to live down. She and her two brothers were mercilessly teased by their peers when they were in that situation.

Besides, living in the valley was like living among extended family, the valley residents were incredibly kind. The community at Bowden Pen had some of the warmest people in the world.

Not to mention the charitable organization, the Farm Help Society that had carried them through the last five years. It was as if that particular charity was looking out for her family exclusively. Everything she owned, even the very clothes on her back now was from the charity.

The charity had been religiously delivering groceries and toiletries every week. And in December, Lucia, her mom and brothers got a full wardrobe for the year. And they were not second-hand clothes. Whoever shopped for them knew them and knew what they liked.

The Farm Help Society had even built them a proper dwelling. She wondered if she should ask them to fix the roof. She didn't want to be a burden, but if they could help she could take out a loan, buy a proper camera lens and maybe a camera stand or two, as well as buy a smaller camera than her Nikon D700...

"Lucia!" her mother had been talking, but she heard not a word. "Are you listening to me?"

"No ma'am," Lucia said truthfully. "I was er... thinking I should write the Farm Help Society and ask for help with the roof."

"Say what now?" Her mother growled. "You didn't hear a word I just said, did you? I already told Dr. Jackson and he said he would fix the roof."

"In exchange for what?" Lucia raised an eyebrow...

OTHER BOOKS BY BRENDA BARRETT

Wiley Brothers Series

Between Brothers (Book 0)- The beginning of the Wiley brothers saga, Joseph Wiley's unconventional family life may prove to be fatal to some members of the family.

For Pete's Sake (Book 1)- Preston has a run in with a child named Pete who claims that he is the grandson of their former housekeeper Pamela Stone.

Crossing Jordan (Book 2)- Jordan is miffed when Shawn takes her new fiancé to Jamaica and insists that he be best man at their wedding.

Fire and Walter (Book 3)- Walter's shady past is affecting his new appointment as church elder. The situation would not only compromise him but a particular newly married church sister as well.

The Perfect Guy (Book 4) - Guy decides to explore the world of farming, becomes an apprentice to a farmer and lives a humble life. He is constantly rebuffed by the woman that he loves because she thinks he is poor!

The Patience of A Saint (Book 5)- Saint attends his own divorce party put on by his soon to be ex wife and they end up complicating matters.

A Case of Love (Book 6)- Case unwittingly buys a bride from a human trafficking ring a few days before his own wedding.

Resetter Series

Never Too Late (Book 1)- Addi finds out she is a resetter and goes back to the summer of 92 to change her family's lives.

Never Say Never (Book 2)- Skyler's handsome college lecturer, who happens to be her neighbor, has a 't' in his palms. Should she tell him the significance of it. If she does, would he believe her?

Now or Never (Book 3)- Ten years later Addi and Randy meet again at Randy's engagement party. Why is it that the chemistry between them was still so potent? Can they ever have a future together? Would Randy choose her this time around?

Almost Never (Book 4)- Tech genius Joshua Porter had all but given up on love. He then meets Portia, an inmate at the female penitentiary and his life takes a turn for the adventurous.

The Scarlett Family Series

Scarlett Baby (Book 1)- When the head of the Scarlett family died, Yuri had to return home to Treasure Beach for the funeral. What he didn't count on was seeing Marla, his childhood sweetheart and his best friend's wife. And when emotions overwhelm them and a few months later Marla is pregnant, Yuri wants the impossible: his best friend's wife and the baby they made together...

Scarlett Sinner (Book 2)- Pastor Troy Scarlett realizes the hard way that some sins are bound to be revealed, like the child that he had out of wedlock with his wife's mortal enemy from college. His wife Chelsea was not happy with the status quo. She was not taking care of the son of the woman she had so despised from college. And she could not get over the deep betrayal that she felt from her husband's indiscretion.

Scarlett Secret (Book 3)- Terri Scarlett had a soft spot for her friend, Lola. She was funny and sweet and they looked remarkably alike. But when Lola's Arab prince demands his bride, Terri foolishly exchange places with her friend and they meet up on a world of trouble.

Scarlett Love (Book 4)- Slater always looked forward to delivering packages to the law firm where he could get a glimpse of the stunning female lawyer, Amoy Gardener. Unfortunately, for Slater a woman like Amoy would not take him seriously, especially when she found out that he could not read!

Scarlett Promise (Book 5)- Driven by desperation Lisa Barclay decides to make some extra money by prostituting herself after being kicked out in the streets. Her first customer turns out to be a popular government senator and then to her horror he dies...

Scarlett Bride (Book 6)- When Oliver Scarlett's missionary work in the Congo region was coming to an end, he had a decision to make, marry Ashaki Azanga and save her from being the fourth wife to the chief of the village or leave her to her fate and get on with his life...

Scarlett Heart (Book 7)- After receiving a heart transplant shy librarian Noah Scarlett started to take on character traits that were unlike him and he kept dreaming of a girl named Cassandra Green...

Rebound Series

On The Rebound- For Better or Worse, Brandon vowed to stay with Ashley, but when worse got too much he moved out and met Nadine. For the first time in years he felt happy, but then Ashley remembered her wedding vows...

On The Rebound 2- Ashley reinvented herself and was now a first lady in a country church in Primrose Hill, but her obsessed ex friend Regina showed up and started digging into the lives of the saints at church. Somebody didn't like Regina's digging. Someone had secrets that were shocking enough to kill for...

Magnolia Sisters

Dear Mystery Guy (Book 1)- Della Gold details her life in a journal dedicated to a mystery guy. But when fascination turns into obsession she finds herself wanting to learn even more about him but in her pursuit of the mystery guy she begins to learn more about herself...

Bad Girl Blues (Book 2)- Brigid Manderson wanted to go to med school but for the time being she was an escort working for her mother, an ex-prostitute. When her latest customer offers her the opportunity of a lifetime would she take it? Or would she choose the harder path and uncertain love with a Christian guy?

Her Mistaken Dreams (Book 3)- Caitlin Denvers dream guy had serious issues. He has a dead wife in his past and he was the main suspect in her murder. Did he really do it? Or did Caitlin for the first time have a mistaken dream?

Just Like Yesterday (Book 4)- Hazel Brown lost six months of memory including the summer that she conceived her son, and had no idea who his father could be. Now that she had the means to fight to get him back from the Deckers, she finds out that the handsome Curtis Decker is willing to share her son with her after all.

New Song Series

Going Solo (Book 1)- Carson Bell, had a lovely voice, a heart of gold, and was no slouch in the looks department. So why did Alice abandon him and their daughter? What did she want after ten years of silence?

Duet on Fire (Book 2)- Ian and Ruby had problems trying to conceive a child. If that wasn't enough, her ex-lover the current pastor of their church wants her back...

Tangled Chords (Book 3)- Xavier Bell, the poor, ugly duckling has made it rich and his looks have been incredibly improved too. Farrah Knight, hotel heiress had cruelly rejected him in the past but now she needed help. Could Xavier forgive and forget?

Broken Harmony(Book 4)- Aaron Lee, wanted the top job in his family company but he had a moral clause to consider just when Alka, his married ex-girlfriend walks back into his life.

A Past Refrain (Book 5)- Jayce had issues with forgetting Haley Greenwald even though he had a new woman in his life. Will he ever be able to shake his love for Haley?

Perfect Melody (Book 6)- Logan Moore had the perfect wife, Melody but his secretary Sabrina was hell bent on breaking up the family. Sabrina wanted Logan whatever the cost and she had a secret about Melody, that could shatter Melody's image to everyone.

The Bancroft Family Series

Homely Girl (Book 0) - April and Taj were opposites in so many ways. He was the cute, athletic boy that everybody wanted to be friends with. She was the overweight, shy, and withdrawn girl. Do April and Taj have a love that can last a lifetime? Or will time and separate paths rip them apart?

Saving Face (Book 1) - Mount Faith University drama begins with a dead president and several suspects including the president in waiting Ryan Bancroft.

Tattered Tiara (Book 2) - Micah Bancroft is targeted by femme fatale Deidra Durkheim. There are also several rape cases to be solved.

Private Dancer (Book 3) Adrian Bancroft was gutted when he returned to Jamaica and found out that his first and only love Cathy Taylor was a stripper and was literally owned by the menacing drug lord, Nanjo Jones.

***Goodbye Lonely (Book 4)* -** Kylie Bancroft was shy and had to resort to going to confidence classes. How could she win the love of Gareth Beecher, her faculty adviser, a man with a jealous ex-wife in his past and a current mystery surrounding a hand found in his garden?

***Practice Run (Book 5)* -** Marcus Bancroft had many reasons to avoid Mount Faith but Deidra Durkheim was not one of them. Unfortunately, on one of his visits he was the victim of a deliberate hit and run.

***Sense of Rumor (Book 6)* -** Arnella Bancroft was the wild, passionate Bancroft, the creative loner who didn't mind living dangerously; but when a terrible thing happened to her at her friend Tracy's party, it changed her. She found that courting rumors can be devastating and that only the truth could set her free.

***A Younger Man (Book 7)*-** Pastor Vanley Bancroft loved Anita Parkinson despite their fifteen-year age gap, but Anita had a secret, one that she could not reveal to Vanley. To tell him would change his feelings toward her, or force him to give up the ministry that he loved so much.

***Just To See Her (Book 8)*-** Jessica Bancroft had the opportunity to meet her fantasy guy Khaled, he was finally coming to Mount Faith but she had feelings for Clay Reid, a guy who had all the qualities she was looking for. Who would she choose and what about the weird fascination Khaled had for Clay?

The Three Rivers Series

Private Sins (Book 1)- Kelly, the first lady at Three Rivers Church was pregnant for the first elder of her church. Could she keep the secret from her husband and pretend that all was well?

Loving Mr. Wright (Book 2)- Erica saw one last opportunity to ditch her single life when Caleb Wright appeared in her town. He was perfect for her, but what was he hiding?

Unholy Matrimony (Book 3) - Phoebe had a problem, she was poor and unhappy. Her solution to marry a rich man was derailed along the way with her feelings for Charles Black, the poor guy next door.

If It Ain't Broke (Book 4)- Chris Donahue wanted a place in his child's life. Pinky Black just wanted his love. She also wanted him to forget his obsession with Kelly and love her. That shouldn't be so hard? Should it?

Contemporary Romance/Drama

*After The End--*Torn between two lovers. Colleen married her high school sweetheart, Isaiah, hoping that they would live happily ever after but life intruded and Isaiah disappeared at sea. She found work with the rich and handsome, Enrique Lopez, as a housekeeper and realized that she couldn't keep him at arms length...

Love Triangle: Three Sides To The Story- George, the husband, Marie, the wife and Karen-the mistress. They all get to tell their side of the story.

The Preacher And The Prostitute - Prostitution and the clergy don't mix. Tell that to ex-prostitute, Maribel, who finds herself in love with the Pastor at her church. Can an ex-prostitute and a pastor have a future together?

New Beginnings - Inner city girl Geneva was offered an opportunity of a lifetime when she found out that her 'real' father was a very wealthy man. Her decision to live up-town meant that she had to leave Froggie, her 'ghetto don,' behind. She also found herself battling with her stepmother and battling her emotions for Justin, a suave up-towner.

Full Circle- After graduating from university, Diana wanted to return to Jamaica to find her siblings. What she didn't foresee was that she would meet Robert Cassidy and that both their pasts would be intertwined, and that disturbing questions would pop up about their parentage, just when they were getting close.

Historical Fiction/Romance

The Empty Hammock- Workaholic, Ana Mendez, fell asleep in a hammock and woke up in the year 1494. It was the time of the Tainos, a time when life seemed simpler, but Ana knew that all of that was about to change.

The Pull Of Freedom- Even in bondage the people, freshly arrived from Africa, considered themselves free. Led by Nanny and Cudjoe the slaves escaped the Simmonds' plantation and went in different directions to forge their destiny in the new country called Jamaica.

Jamaican Comedy (Material contains Jamaican dialect)

Di Taxi Ride And Other Stories- Di Taxi Ride and Other Stories is a collection of twelve witty and fast paced short stories. Each story tells of a unique slice of Jamaican life.